An Australian Historical Romance

Home is the Heart

LENA WEST

Gymea Publishing

Published by Gymea Publishing

https://www.facebook.com/LenaWestAuthor/

www.lenawestauthor.com

ISBN-13: 978-0-6485978-1-0

Disclaimer

This story is a work of fiction.

Names, characters, places and incidents are the product of the author's imagination and are used fictitiously. Any resemblance to events, locales or actual persons, living or dead, is entirely coincidental.

Some actual persons and locations are referenced in passing.

Table of Contents

Dedication

To Darryl. He was with me when I picked up a gold-flecked shard under the sign announcing the first discovery of gold in Western Australia – in Golden Valley near Southern Cross.

Acknowledgements

Special thanks go to New Norcia archivist, Peter Hocking, who provided me with the answers to several questions I had regarding the New Norcia community in 1890.

He also sent me a brief biography of Fr Bernado Martinez, a real person (along with Abbot Rosendo Salvado) who plays a small but pivotal role in my story. By a wonderful coincidence, Fr Martinez was, in real life, exactly the kind and gentle person I wanted him to be in my purely fictional story.

HOME IS THE HEART

1

Perth, March, 1888

"Eliza! Eliza, I've 'eard the most amazin' news!"

So excited he forgot the careful enunciation he usually tried to copy from his wife, Jason Baker, wavy brown hair in its usual state of disarray, burst into their bedroom where Eliza, only just returned herself, sat waiting for him.

Just yesterday, along with a group of other new immigrants who had crossed the world on the same ship, they had travelled up the Swan River to Perth, from the port of Freemantle where they had disembarked the day before. Advised there would be more opportunities for both of them to find work in the larger town, they had settled into this lodging house in the interim.

It had been a shock to Eliza to find the city of Perth all new and raw compared to her old home in Manchester, but the people she had met were lovely; so friendly and helpful she felt buoyed up by optimism. Although she had failed to find work during the day, she had a list of other businesses to approach the on the morrow.

"Have you found work, then, Jason? Already? How wonderful."

Eliza ran to her husband, clapping her hands in delight.

Thrilled to the core with his exciting news, Jason lifted Eliza off her feet, twirling her round and round till, laughing and beginning to feel giddy, she begged him to set her back on her feet. A bit unsteady, she clung to him, gazing adoringly, trustingly, into his beloved face.

"Not work, my love. Even better. An opportunity! Ye'll never guess, Eliza."

He wrapped his arms around his lovely young wife, seizing the moment to steal a kiss. Sometimes he still found it difficult to believe he'd been lucky enough to win the heart of Eliza Harris.

"Jason, whatever do you mean?"

Emerging from her husband's kiss, Eliza pushed back to study his face, alive and glowing with excitement as she'd never seen it before. Infected by his enthusiasm, a corresponding excitement began to fizz in her veins. She sank back onto the bed where she had been sitting, tugging Jason down beside her.

"Tell me quickly, Jason. What could possibly be better than finding a good job on your first day of looking? What's got you all het up?"

One hand holding Eliza's, Jason leaned forward, eager to share his news.

"It's gold, darlin'," he whispered, voice lowered so no-one passing by outside could overhear. "Gold! Just think on it, Eliza. They're diggin' gold outta the ground at a place called Southern Cross."

Eyes aglow with excitement, he explained, "It's there fer the takin', Lizzie darlin', fer anyone who's prepared ta dig fer it. All yer need is a licence, then yer can pick yer spot and stake a claim."

A disquieting chill feathered down Eliza's spine.

"Where did you hear this, Jason? Are you sure you've got it right? What if we go haring off to this Southern Cross place and find the gold is all run out? Or the good claims have all been taken?"

Eliza thought for a moment. Jason was a good man, the best. She wouldn't have married him otherwise. But she didn't trust this talk of gold. Didn't believe their fortune could be made so easily.

"I've been askin' around."

Jason grinned. He knew his Eliza. Pretty as a picture she was, with her trim figure, yellow hair done up in a prim bun and trusting blue eyes. She'd captured his heart the moment he'd set eyes on her. He liked the way she kept him on an even keel, considering her cautious nature the perfect foil to his own impetuosity. This time though, his eyes blinded by gold-lust, he set about convincing her his new dream was at least a possibility.

"Seems the first gold was discovered in 1887. Only just over a year ago, Eliza. Round about the time we were gettin' ourselves married, but they're only now startin' to get organised. If we go right away Lizzie darlin', we'll be in at the start, afore the big companies start buyin' the little miners up. I met up wiv a chap called George Sampson. He's been chasin' gold from California to New South Wales and now 'ere."

Jason slowed to catch his breath.

"George knows what ta look fer. I'll take ye ta meet him tomorra and ye can hear it fer yerself."

Jason gave Eliza a little shake, then rattled on, not giving her the chance to get a word in edgewise.

"He's promised to tell us 'ow to go about it if we're interested. He's found several fortunes, 'e said, and lost 'em all through foolishness. This time he's plannin' to set 'imself up for 'is old age. Reckons if we 'ave a go and do well, we'll be set up, too. Fer life, Eliza. Just think. If we don't, then we come back 'ere and look for work, just as we planned. Either way, we won't lose out, and we might just end up rich. All fer a bit o' hard work. We can do it, Lizzie. We can an' all."

Eliza nodded her head, glad to see Jason hadn't quite lost all touch with reality. She had been staring at him, open mouthed, as he talked. Listening and taking it all in. She loved him so much, this strong, energetic young man who had swept her off her feet, persuading her to marry him and emigrate with him half-way round the world to Western Australia.

Initially, Eliza hadn't really wanted to leave Manchester, let alone England. It was her home, the only one she'd ever known. Western Australia had seemed so frighteningly alien and far away. Finally, with the onset of a miserable English winter, the promise of sunshine and blue skies, and Jason's persistence, had won her over. Now, the idea of Jason's proposed treasure hunt churning in her brain, she gazed expectantly into his eager brown eyes.

Jason Baker couldn't really be termed handsome, she thought indulgently.

Unlike Donald Sykes, the fiancé who had jilted her almost two years earlier. When her mother's death from consumption hard on the heels of her father's accidental death, had left her a penniless orphan, she had turned to Donald, fully trusting him to take care of her, only to be let down in the worst possible manner.

For the longest time she had bitterly resented Donald's defection; the more so when she learned he had slyly been courting the daughter of a wealthy businessman while she had been caught up in the heart-rending, unsuccessful struggle to save her mother's life. Until she fell in love with Jason, she had been unable to acknowledge, even to herself, that it had been her pride, more than her heart, which Donald had damaged. Now Jason Baker was her whole world.

Fondly, she smiled, filling her eyes with his quite ordinary face, sprinkled with a homely dash of freckles across the bridge of his snub nose. How much more she preferred the heartfelt honesty and integrity which shone so brightly in Jason's sparkling brown eyes. She'd never be taken in by traitorous good looks again.

The dinner gong rang before she could think what answer to give Jason about the gold, and they descended silently, hand in hand, to the dining room. It was almost impossible to think of anything else. Each privately mulling over the scheme, they concentrated on their food, afterwards returning directly to their room to continue the discussion out of hearing of their fellow lodgers. It was quite late when they finished thrashing out a mutually acceptable plan and set about getting ready for bed.

*****

Brooding over their plans to spend the following day gathering information on prospecting, and the gold discoveries taking place in the East of the Colony, Eliza sat brushing her hair, soon becoming distracted by the view in the mirror of her husband sitting on the bed behind her.

Absent-mindedly, she admired the way the Indian Ocean sunshine had gilded the tips of Jason's unruly, light brown curls. His skin had acquired a tan from spending every minute he could in the blazing sunshine during the long voyage across the vast ocean. Too restless for staid promenading around the decks, he'd fallen into the habit of helping the sailors in their endless tasks, often bare-armed as they were. She thought he looked as tough and weathered as the sun-bronzed colonial men she'd seen in the town. Australians, as they called themselves.

Watching Jason, the sight of those bare, brown arms and sinewy muscles sent her pulse racing. Her breath hitched in her throat. Her eyes slanted sideways to the bed they would soon be sharing, and a blush staining her cheeks, thought of lying there in her Jason's arms. Her husband's arms.

Catching her watching him, Jason's lips curled into a devilish grin promising those delights which were still so new to her. Delights she knew she would never tire of. Or have enough of. Jason rose to his feet, coming to stand at her back, trailing his strong, lean hands down her arms. A delicious tension began coiling in the pit of her stomach.

Bending to graze her temple with his lips, Jason took the brush from her fingers and finished brushing out her long, golden ringlets. He loved the sensuous feel of the long tresses sliding through his fingers.

He loved Eliza.

Loved being married to her.

It had been nothing short of a miracle for an orphan from the London slums to win the love of the gently-born girl who had become his wife. Every day Jason silently renewed his vow to improve himself; to become worthy of her.

Right now, eager as he was to have her beneath him in their bed, he couldn't resist the exquisite torment of forcing himself to wait, just a little longer. He dropped a lingering kiss onto the top of her head, the reflected smile it earned him setting a slow burn simmering in his blood.

Eliza sighed with pleasure at the feel of Jason's hands stroking her hair. Nerve ends tingling, and eager as she was for the satisfaction which would soon be hers, still, she felt too disturbed by the earlier conversation to relax completely and surrender to her husband's ministrations.

"You seem really set on going after this gold, Jason?"

She swivelled round on the stool to talk face-to-face, a slight frown creasing her smooth, white forehead.

"Are you so very sure it's the right thing for us to do?"

Irrational fear roiled in her stomach every time she thought about it, but with no valid objection to make, she was not willing to let it cause trouble between the two of them.

She hadn't been married to Jason for long enough to predict his reaction if she set herself steadfastly in opposition to his wishes. However, she really couldn't like the uncertainty of the scheme.

There had been far too much uncertainty in her life in recent years, culminating in the huge risk they had taken of emigrating to this strange, new land in search of a better life. She was very much afraid she lacked her husband's boundless enthusiasm and daring.

Jason looked into the open, honest blue of Eliza's eyes, reading the worry she couldn't hide. Genuine anxiety clouded their depths.

He bit back the easy reassurance which sprang to his lips.

He couldn't lie.

Not to the sweetest, most important person in his life. Eliza deserved nothing less than the truth from him. He wasn't on his own any more, making spur-of-the-moment decisions which only affected himself. He had to consider both of them now.

Love for Eliza had filled the emptiness which had lain for so many years at the centre of his being, yet marriage carried heavy responsibilities he was still coming to terms with. An unfamiliar pensiveness wiped the smile from his face.

"No," he finally said, so softly Eliza barely heard the word. Voice firming, he resolutely continued.

"No, Eliza darlin, I'm not at all sure and certain it's the right thing. What I am sure of is; if I turn my back on this once-in-a-lifetime opportunity, I'll always regret not givin' it a try."

And resent me for holding you back?

In the silence of her mind Eliza added the unspoken rider. A nebulous dread darkened her spirits.

Her Scottish grandmother had claimed to have 'the sight', and once or twice she herself had thought she might have had true premonitions.

Premonitions of disaster, such as the terrible fear which had assailed her one morning while watching her father leave for work. Tempted to call him back, she later wished she had, since that had been the last time she had seen him alive.

This feeling tonight didn't have the same sharp sense of urgency, so maybe it was no more than natural trepidation engendered by the unknown. She prayed it was no more. Forcing a shaky smile to lips suddenly turned cold and unresponsive, she nodded.

Jason leaned down, his lips claiming hers in the tenderest of kisses.

"I want ta give ye a good life, wiv all the comforts ye deserve, Eliza me darlin'. The children we'll be havin', too, God willin'; and this is a heaven-sent opportunity. It'll be hard work fer sure, but it takes more'n hard work ta scare me."

He could still read an uncertainty she struggled to hide from him.

"I can see ye have reservations, though, love. If you're dead set against it, I'll give up the idea right this minute and we'll say no more about it. Your happiness is more important than a dream of riches."

Jason pressed his lips to hers once more, in a kiss which felt to Eliza like a solemn promise. Her heart melted, and she kissed him back, her tongue slipping between his parted lips to stroke the inside of his mouth in blatant invitation.

To think this man loved her so much he'd give up his dreams for her, just because she was a silly little scaredy-cat, afraid of taking a risk.

I can't ask it of him. Won't. Eliza reached deep for the courage to abide by her decision. *Not when he's doing it for me as much as himself.*

She swallowed, forcing her fears into a tiny corner of her mind.

Instead of trampling on Jason's dreams, she would wholeheartedly do everything within her power to help her man achieve success. A success worked for and shared by them both.

"It's all right, Jason darling," she murmured. "I'm just being silly, letting a woman's foolish fears stand in our way. Let's go dig some gold. Tomorrow. I have other plans for tonight."

*****

Much later that same night, Eliza lay awake, her husband sleeping in her arms. She stroked his curls back from his forehead, careful not to wake him.

The day she met Jason Baker had been the luckiest day of her life. Everything changed for Eliza that Sunday morning when she stumbled on the rough steps outside her church; literally falling into Jason Baker's strong arms when he stepped forward to catch her.

She had noticed him slipping into a pew in the back of the small church, several weeks in a row, however this was the first time they had met.

In later weeks, as she had come to know him for the honest, stalwart young man he was, she had come to think he had been Heaven-sent.

When he rescued her from falling, her heart had beaten faster at the intimate feel of his arms supporting her against his chest, but she had persuaded herself it was the shock of her near accident, not the man. He had fallen into step beside her, chatting as he escorted her back to the Widow Jenkins' house where she rented a room, and it had felt to Eliza as if the sun shone brightly, even though the weather was dull and gusty, with rain threatening.

All through summer they had walked out together. Sunday became the highlight of Eliza's week. Not because it was God's day, but because Sunday was the day she saw Jason Baker.

One Sunday afternoon as they followed the path beside the river, he told her of a lecture he planned to attend in the church hall on the following Wednesday evening. A friend of the Vicar was going to talk about a faraway corner of the Empire called Western Australia. A land abounding in strange animals called kangaroos, and flocks of improbably coloured wild parakeets.

"Ye oughta come wiv me, Lizzie. There's goin' ta be tea and biscuits at the end, and we can ask questions, too. It'll be fun."

Eliza hadn't cared tuppence about the lecture, but since it meant extra hours in Jason's company, she agreed immediately.

That night marked a change in Jason. Eliza noticed he became purposeful, talking about the future, and how he wanted to improve himself.

He made frequent references to Western Australia and the abundant opportunities it offered a man willing to work hard to do well for himself. Opportunities lacking in England.

The day he told her he had decided to emigrate, she had wept in his arms, fearing she would never see him again. She had only just found him, and she was about to lose him forever.

That was the day she realised she loved Jason Baker with a woman's love.

"Dearest Eliza," he had said, drying his cheeks with his handkerchief, "Don't cry. I didn't mean ta make yer cry. Listen. Hear me out, will yer? Please?"

Sitting beside her on the park bench overlooking the river, he clasped her hands in his, smiling when she obediently turned her face up to him, valiantly holding back her tears.

"I mean the both of us, Lizzie darlin'. I want ye ta come ta Western Australia wiv me." He blushed, gulped, and said the sweetest words she had ever heard.

"I love ye, Eliza. I want ta marry ye. Please say ye will. We can get married and go ta seek our fortunes in Western Australia together. How about it, Lizzie darlin'?

Agreeing to marry Jason was the easy part.

Agreeing to emigrate half-way around the world took considerably more persuasion, but, love outweighing fear, she had agreed.

Now they were here, and a new adventure loomed, threatening to overturn their carefully laid plans.

Their happiness still had the feel of a fairytale come to life, and Eliza didn't regret marrying Jason. Not for one moment; but, oh, how she hoped he'd settle down when he got this gold-fever out of his system. She didn't really believe they would strike it rich, but she would follow him on one more big adventure, then she wanted a home of their own.

She yearned for a settled life.

For a home; and a family.

Is it really so much to ask? Eliza prayed it wasn't.

HOME IS THE HEART

2

The Jackson Farm, Spring, 1887.

Way past his usual knocking off time, Sean O'Grady lifted the ragged work-hat from damp black hair, wiping his forearm wearily across his sweaty brow. The heat was cruel, but planting up the paddocks had to be completed today if they were to take advantage of the predicted rain. Anyway, it was finished, and just in time, judging by the clouds gathering to the south. It looked very much as if the weather pundits were right for once.

Tomorrow looked like being a day to sit back, watch the rain fall, and take a break. A day to spend relaxing in the company of his wife and children. A dusty smile lightened Sean's tired face, and renewed energy put a spring in his step as he mounted to the front porch of their cottage.

"Sean! You're here at last. I've got water heated for your bath, but you'll have to hurry, or we'll be late, and you don't want that."

"Don't nag, Ann my darling."

Although her husband's endearment brought an indulgent smile to Ann O'Grady's lips, despite the words preceding it, her hands continued to wave him urgently towards their tiny cottage's lean-to annexe where hot water steamed in the laundry copper and she had set out the tin tub they used for bathing.

Kicking his scuffed, dusty boots off on the porch, Sean took in his wife's clean, fresh appearance, remembering they were due at the main house for dinner tonight. His Ann was so pretty, with the soft chestnut curls and warm, dark brown eyes she had bequeathed to their daughters. Such a delicious armful. Sean's pulse, and a certain other portion of his anatomy, quickened. After the little ones were safely tucked up in bed he'd … A sensuous smile conveyed his thoughts to his wife, bringing rosy colour to her cheeks and a sly smile to her lips

Thank the good Lord she's a hot-blooded woman a man can enjoy taking to his bed, Sean thought. Not for the first time.

"Please, love. Hurry up!"

Ann might be laughing, but Sean knew her well enough to know she meant what she said. Recalling where they were going, he sobered up. He very definitely didn't want to be late.

"I'll not share my dirt, love, but I'll be through the bath and into my Sunday best all the quicker with one of your sweet kisses to speed me on my way."

And I'll keep that other sweet thought in my mind for when we're home again.

He puckered up, and Ann, laughing at his nonsense, obligingly leaned forward, her lips lingering on his for an extra-long moment.

"You too, girls. I need kisses from you two as well."

Sean winked at his daughters, chuckling at their giggling attempts to wink back at him which involved a great deal of scrunching up of their beloved infant faces. Crouching down, he ostentatiously scrubbed clean a patch on either cheek to receive his daughters' moist babyish kisses.

Some men yearned for sons, but Sean O'Grady wouldn't trade a single hair from the head of either little girl for a cricket team of sons. Born of the love he and Ann shared, three-year-old Mary and one-year-old Judy were treasures beyond price.

Lowering himself gingerly into the steaming tub a short time later, he reminded himself to hurry up. *For Ann's sake,* he thought. *Augusta Jackson hardly needs an added excuse to find fault with me. My very existence is fault enough.*

Even though it was due to his agricultural expertise the woman enjoyed such a comfortable life, a mere farm manager would never have been good enough for her only child. It didn't matter that he and Ann loved each other. Or that Augusta's husband, Humphrey Jackson, had given the match his unqualified blessing. Five years after Ann married him, Augusta still berated her daughter at every opportunity for throwing away her matrimonial chances. When Sean was within earshot, she could be counted on to be especially scornful.

Augusta's tongue, Sean mused, *can cut a man down to nothing faster than a hot knife sliding through butter.*

Usually he turned a deaf ear, quietly revelling in the knowledge being ignored was anathema to his mother-in-law. Unfortunately, she no longer confined herself to picking on him. Lately her vitriol was aimed equally at Ann and the children. His lips tightened in anger.

She better not start on them tonight!

But I better not dawdle, either, or it'll be my Annie who suffers most.

Feeling the stiffness and knotted muscles caused by hard work easing under the soothing caress of warm bath water, Sean wished he could afford to linger. But Augusta found plenty of fuel for complaint without his handing her more for free.

*****

"Mary and Judith, my darlings. How about a big hug and a kiss for your old Grandpapa?"

Humphrey, emerging onto the verandah to meet them, held his arms wide. Catching Mary up for the requested hug and kiss, he twirled her round and round until her giddy laughter alerted his wife to the arrival of their guests. Her yappy little pug, Shadow, at her heels as usual, Augusta swept onto the verandah.

"Put that child down, you fool," she snapped. "Before you make her so dizzy she sicks up all over you."

"Now, now, Augusta." Humphrey, slowing to answer his wife, gave his granddaughter an extra hug and a quick tickle. "You know very well our Mary hasn't done that for at least two years. You're a big girl now, aren't you love?"

This last was directed to the child in his arms. Nonetheless, he set her back on her feet.

"My turn, Gran'papa. My turn." Judith lisped, raising chubby arms.

While Humphrey gave his younger granddaughter a slightly less vigorous, but no less loving, greeting, Ann straightened her back and stepped forward to greet her mother.

"Mama," she murmured, kissing the air beside her mother's cheek.

"Augusta." Sean's nod and curt greeting held no pretence of affection. He was careful to always be polite, but the antipathy between the two of them was entirely mutual.

"Humph!" Less polite, Augusta tilted her chin disdainfully and gave Sean her shoulder.

The cold one, he thought irreverently, not that either was particularly warm, whoever you happened to be.

"Mama." Ann stepped between her husband and mother. "These are for you. From my garden." She tendered a large bouquet of the native everlasting daisies which cheerfully proliferated in her garden in front of the cottage. Tied with a blue ribbon, they were so pretty they'd bring a smile to most faces. But not Augusta's.

"Whatever are you bringing me those rubbishing weeds for? When I want cut flowers, I can get much better from my own garden."

Sean, seeing his wife's lips quiver, felt angry heat flooding through his veins. He took a step forward, but his father-in-law's glare halted him in his tracks.

Humphrey, handing Judy into her father's arms, stepped forward, sweeping Ann into an enveloping hug and kissing her soundly on both cheeks.

"Your daisies may not be fancy enough for your mother, Ann dear, but I love them, and I'm claiming these for my study. Every time I look at them, I'll be thinking of you, my darling."

"Humph!" Augusta, cheeks red with either fury or shame, and Sean was willing to bet the former, snorted. "What are you all standing about for, anyway? Dinner's ready. If you'd been any longer getting here, Cook would have been complaining her roast lamb was overdone."

Turning abruptly, she flung the door wide and stalked off inside, the others following meekly on her heels.

"Sorry. As you know, your mother's a difficult woman, darling," Humphrey whispered in his daughter's ear.

A wobbly smile, curving her mouth up at the corners, Ann nodded.

Humphrey's statement was nothing new to anyone who knew Augusta Jackson.

And we haven't even sat down yet. For two pins, Sean would remove his family, not just from this house, this farm, but from the entire neighbourhood. As far from his mother-in-law's poisonous influence as possible. Unfortunately, to do so would be to punish Humphrey unfairly, and he owed that good, decent and loving man too much to hurt him so.

*****

" and thank you, God, for the food we are about to eat. Amen."

20

And thank you, darling Mary, Sean added in his mind as, out of deeply ingrained habit, he joined in with the 'Amen.' When Augusta had demanded her granddaughter say grace, he'd seen Ann tense, as the little girl sometimes had a unique take on her prayers which he and Ann found charming, but Augusta could be counted on to take exception to. However, even the most critical of grandmothers would have found Mary's simple litany of thanks for family, friends and food entirely acceptable. Now they could all relax and get on with the meal the Jackson's cook was serving.

"This shoulder of lamb is excellent, my dear. Excellent." Humphrey helped himself liberally to the mint sauce while Ann and Sean unobtrusively aided their daughters by cutting their meat into bite-sized pieces.

"Would someone pass the peas, please?"

Breaking off what he was doing, Sean, closest to the dish of peas, obliged, passing it down the table to Augusta, though he couldn't help wishing she'd just once speak *to* him instead of *at* him. Duty done, he finished cutting up Mary's slice of roast lamb.

"Ann!"

Augusta's strident tone brought the whole family to attention, waiting to hear her complaint. Because they well knew that particular tone invariably signalled a fault found. Sighing resignedly, Ann turned to face her mother.

"Yes, Mama?"

"Why is *he* cutting that child's meat? I thought you told me just yesterday she could handle her knife and fork for herself."

"*He,*" Sean impatiently pre-empted his wife's answer, unable to resist emphasising his mother-in-law's rudeness this time, "is cutting Mary's food, because, although she can most certainly handle *her own* child-sized knife and fork, these heavy utensils made for adult hands are too awkward for her tiny hands to manage. Unless, of course, you wish to risk having gravy splashed all over your fine Irish linen tablecloth. Next time I'll remember to bring the children's own cutlery."

Silence reigned, the children and other adults holding their breath, waiting for Sean's insubordination to send Augusta into an apoplexy. No-one crossed Augusta Jackson. No-one except Sean, who boldly outstared her.

"Humph!"

Tense shoulders relaxed, and all six people seated at the table applied themselves to their plates.

That exchange set the tone for the rest of the meal. Their self-protective instincts kicking in, the children remained silent unless invited to speak. A desultory conversation flowed between the adults, and if it was at times rather stilted, at least it was safe.

Only Sean played with fire, deliberately, with a sunny, open smile, politely directing innocuous comments and questions to Augusta.

Only Ann, kicking him under the table, seemed to appreciate what he was up to. But Sean, winking reassurance, knew exactly what he was doing. He subtly diverted Augusta's wrath onto himself, thereby sparing Ann and the girls from any further ordeals. And every time he reduced his prey to "Humph!", he considered it a victory.

When he forced her to answer him in actual words, it was an even sweeter victory.

By the time the men retired to the side verandah with their cigars and port, Sean was worn to the bone from the evening's battle.

Can't the bloody woman see she's got a whole family who want to love her? Really and truly? Can't she see she's destroying her own best chance of happiness, pushing them away with her carping and nagging?

The speed with which Sean downed his drink was an insult to the fine port Humphrey stocked. Wordlessly, he accepted a second glass. Sighing, he wished someone would sit Augusta down and talk some sense into her. His eyes turned to Humphrey, his mouth opening to voice his opinion, but he changed his mind. Gentle and peaceable, Humphrey was no match for his harridan of a wife.

HOME IS THE HEART

3

Perth to Southern Cross.

Several days passed before Eliza and Jason set out for the goldfields. Days spent under George Sampson's guidance learning about the methods employed in extracting gold from the earth, buying the few basic tools they would need, and the other equipment essential for life in a mining camp. Such as water containers, cast iron pots and pans for cooking over an open fire, bedrolls for sleeping on the ground and a tent to shelter them from the elements.

The list seemed endless. Since their pockets were far from bottomless, and they weren't planning to be gold prospectors forever, they cut their shopping list to the bare bones.

Even so, George considered it a good investment to purchase a horse and a small two-wheeled cart.

"We have to get there first, lugging all this stuff," George explained.

"We've got too much to carry on our backs for such a great distance, but it'll all be far more expensive if we wait till we arrive to buy it. Some fellows use wheelbarrows, but with a horse and cart we'll get there quicker, and I'll sell them easy enough at the other end. Probably for a decent profit."

"Well, George," Eliza sighed, stowing the last of her bundles into the cart, "I for one, am very grateful to Hercules here. There's no way I could have carried my share of this load. Thank goodness your pockets are deeper than ours." She patted the placid animal, feeding him a piece of carrot.

Last night, Eliza had done her sums carefully, shocked to discover the dangerously low ebb their finances had fallen to. They damned well better find gold, or they would never have the money to return and start again. Entering into a partnership with the more experienced George Sampson gave Eliza a boost in confidence, however. George made absolutely everything seem so simple and straightforward and his boundless enthusiasm was contagious.

*****

In spirits so high it felt almost like a holiday, they set out at first light, walking alongside the cart to save the horse.

"Just look at me, Jason," Eliza laughed, holding her arms wide as she danced along the street at his side. "With a man's hat and boots, I look a real country bumpkin. I'm glad no-one I know can see me now."

"Not a country bumpkin, Eliza dear. A gold miner's wife, and thet's altogether different," Jason grinned. "Ye'll be the prettiest miner in Southern Cross, thet ye will."

"You'll be glad of that wide brim as the day heats up, my girl, and your normal shoes would fall to pieces long before we arrive," George was quick to remind her.

A cheerful smile on her face, Eliza agreed, although sometimes she thought her face would crack from all the smiling she'd been doing to hide her fears behind a happy facade. She would be no help to Jason whatever if she went about like a scared chicken, and she was determined to make her husband proud of her. If this venture failed, it wouldn't be because *she* lacked spirit.

With the last houses behind them, and nothing but the long, dusty road ahead, conversation dwindled to the odd desultory remark. Unused to such exercise, both Bakers began to feel the strain, but George, checking the map, insisted on going a little further before allowing his companions to take a rest.

"We can't afford to keep on having rests every half hour or so. It's still a long way to go before we reach the first camping spot. If we don't get there today, we won't be able to refill the water bottles," he reminded them. "We'll take a break in another half an hour. Come on, Eliza, step it out. Don't dawdle."

Eliza glared daggers at George's back, muttering under her breath about insensitive males, but she stepped it out as ordered.

The two hundred and thirty something miles to Southern Cross began to seem an impossible distance. Eliza did mental calculations involving distance, speed and provisions as they plodded on.

A shiver rippled down her spine, belying the heat of the day when she came up short every time.

Following the rutted wheel tracks that passed for a road, they left the town behind in the heat haze. There were none of the friendly little villages every mile or two there would have been in England. This truly was a vast, alien land, with dry, brown grass and a great bowl of a burnished, shimmering blue sky beating down on them. Eliza had to bite her tongue to hold in a demand to turn back. Too tired to keep on smiling, she reached for Jason's hand, drawing strength from her husband whose adventurous spirit remained undimmed.

"Don't argue, girl. Hop up on the cart and give your feet a rest."

George had been watching, carefully gauging Eliza's strength. "You don't want those new boots to rub blisters. In a few days you'll be walking as briskly as us, but till then you need to be a bit careful-like."

Eliza thanked the Good Lord for small mercies, and scrambled up behind Hercules.

When they finally reached the camp, she was so weary she could barely keep her eyes open to help prepare supper. The next day was little better, but by the time they had climbed to the top of the Darling Escarpment, the low range to the east of Perth, they were all growing accustomed to the daily slog. At least the landscape had grown more interesting with the track winding through stands of magnificent forest trees instead of the sparse, scrubby vegetation of the first day.

Looking at George's map while they sat round the campfire, Eliza couldn't help herself.

"Have we only come that tiny distance?" she exclaimed. "I know it's hundreds of miles to Southern Cross, but I was sure we'd be further along by now."

She was appalled by how short a distance they had travelled; and what a terribly long way still lay ahead of them.

George laughed, "Don't take it like that lass. We've made good time, and we'll do better from here on. It's downhill all the way now, don'tcha know? Just think how fit we'll all be when we arrive."

"We're not alone any longer, either," Jason noted, silently counting the tiny campfires scattered throughout the clearing carved out of the forest. They were now part of a growing band of people straggling east, lured on by the siren call of gold. Very few people they encountered were going in the opposite direction. A couple of days later George pointed towards a huddle of buildings in the distance.

"There it is folks. Northam. The last town of any size before Southern Cross. We'll rest for a day to catch up on a few chores and replenish our supplies," he added.

"Hooray!" Wide grins split the men's faces at Eliza's heartfelt cheer.

Plodding on again, Eliza and Jason looked at each other, the same thought running through both of their minds. They were going to do this. They were going to succeed. If they stayed strong.

Northam, which they knew fell far short of their final destination, looked barely big enough to be called a village, let alone the sizeable town George claimed it to be!

29

All the same, the idea of a rest from the interminable road was more than welcome.

"You know Jason. Later, when we're ready to settle down, this might be a place to consider."

Eliza gazed thoughtfully about, studying the rural landscape as they neared the town. Their path led them between fields of stubble where grain had been recently harvested. Further over a farmer followed a sturdy horse, guiding his plough, a dust plume streaming out behind in the light breeze. Farmhouses were scattered across the valley which held the town at its centre, and a stream they later learnt was the Avon River, snaked its way across the valley bottom.

"Na, I don't think so darlin'." Jason stood a moment considering her suggestion. "It's good country right enough. As well as I can judge, leastways, only I'm no farmer. I wouldn't know where ta start."

He shook his head, dismissing the idea. Laughing, Eliza took his hand in both of hers, leaning into his shoulder.

"I know that, Jason Love. I didn't mean we should become farmers."

"What then?" Jason, unlike most men of his time, would be the first to acknowledge his wife's intelligence and sound common sense, and, liking the look of the countryside as much as she did, was becoming curious as to what she meant.

"A farming community needs all sorts of services, Jason. I was thinking of a shop. You could find work that interests you and I could mind the shop."

Eliza smiled, drifting off into a daydream of the idyllic future awaiting them. Jason turned the idea over in his mind as they hurried to catch up with George and the cart, liking it more and more. He stopped and swung Eliza up in his arms, twirling her round and round. Setting her back on her feet, he surprised her with a smacking kiss.

"We'll do it love. When we find gold, we'll buy a nice little shop for you and I'll set up as a carpenter like I was trained for. Right here in Northam, or somewhere similar."

Jason whistled a jaunty tune, accompanying Eliza's singing as they walked along, swinging their clasped hands between them.

Even though the town was smaller than they'd expected, the sight of prosperous farmlands cheered the whole party. Even better was not having to walk further than the main street the next morning. When they did set off again, Eliza was amazed at the ease with which she kept up during the long days, falling into a steady rhythm.

Her legs had strengthened, just as George had assured her they would. Now she had the energy to study the terrain as they passed through, she began to realise these Australian woodlands, so vastly different to those in England, had a distinctive, subtle beauty all their own. Even so, she almost lost count of the days spent on the road before reaching their final destination.

HOME IS THE HEART

4

The Jackson Farm, May, 1888.

Whistling off-key, Sean rubbed down his horse and added a scoop of oats to the hay in its manger. The fancifully named Prince Valiant, Prince to all and sundry, deserved an extra treat today. The small herd of prime beasts he and his men had driven to the saleyards had been feisty enough to keep them all on their toes.

With a last fond slap on the horse's hindquarters, Sean set off across the home paddock to his cottage. Tucked into a sheltered nook behind a mulga clump, it was out of sight from the main house, for which he and Ann gave thanks to God. It was bad enough Augusta felt entitled to invade their privacy whenever she pleased, without their every move being open to her scrutiny. Of course, it was Ann who bore the brunt of her mother's nosiness. Augusta knew better than to get in *his* way.

Thinking of Ann and his girls, Sean patted his pockets.

Leaving his men to go ahead, he'd detoured via the shops on his ride home. Lollipops for Mary and Judy jostled the silk-wrapped mother-of-pearl combs he'd found for Ann. Usually one had to venture all the way into Perth for such exotic oriental treasures, but today had been his lucky day. Stopping suddenly, he frowned.

Where were his girls?

In the afternoons they habitually watched for his return, running out to meet him and take turns to ride home on his shoulders. He pulled out his watch to check the time. Of course. Today he was earlier than usual. It didn't really matter, of course, but he did so look forward to their enthusiastic greetings. He walked a little quicker, eager to reach home.

Stepping up onto the porch, the sound of his wife's sobbing reached his ears, sending a cold chill to his heart.

"Ann! Ann, darling!" he called, bursting through the door to throw himself down at his wife's feet. "What is it? Is someone hurt? One of the girls? What can I do?"

Ann's watery attempt at a reassuring smile was pitiful. She sniffed back her sobs.

"Oh, Sean. I'm so glad you're home at last." Her arms were wrapped around her daughters on either side of her on the sofa, otherwise she would have thrown herself into his arms.

Running frantic eyes over his 'three ladies' as he liked to call them, Sean could detect no visible signs of injury except for one of Mary's cheeks which sported a red mark darkening into what would be a substantial bruise by bedtime.

"What happened to Mary?"

Not wanting to add to the emotional turmoil, he deliberately kept his tone even, merely reaching gentle fingers to the girl's injured cheek, wincing inwardly when she flinched away.

"Shh, baby." Ann released Judy to pull Mary onto her lap, pressing the girl's head down against her breast. "Shhh. Papa's here. Everything's all right now."

But everything was so obviously *not* all right.

Kneeling, Sean enveloped all three of them in his comforting embrace. Anger began bubbling beneath his seemingly placid exterior. He opened his mouth to give voice to the questions whirling through his brain, shutting it again when Ann lay restraining fingers against his lips.

"I'll tell you, darling. In just a wee minute. Girls, will you be good now, while I talk to Papa outside?"

Rising to her feet, she held out her hand to her husband, leaving her daughters huddled together, little Judy offering the comfort of her tiny arms to her big sister.

Remembering his gifts, Sean produced the lollipops.

"I brought these back from town for you, my darlings. Now, dry up those tears while Mama and I talk."

If the sweets didn't result in the tears magically disappearing, they certainly helped tiny rainbow smiles to peek through the storm.

"Thank you, Papa," the girls chorused.

"Good girls."

Sean kissed the tops of their heads and stepped outside to where Ann waited on the porch.

"Let's take a walk." Taking Sean's hand, Ann led him into the garden. Holding himself in, Sean waited till she was ready to speak.

"Mama visited today." She slanted a glance sideways, taking in his tight lips. Stony-voiced, she continued. "She comes every day, and usually stays far too long, since all she does is complain about the girls for one thing or another. Or find fault with the way I conduct my household. Or harp on about the chances I threw away when I married you."

She gripped Sean's hand, drawing him to a halt.

"She's wrong, Sean. Marrying you is the best thing I've ever done. And it's *my* house. I'll do things *my* way in my own home. Mama doesn't have any right to come here trying to take over. And our girls are good girls, Sean. You know they are. If they need to be disciplined, I'll do it. Or you will. It's not *her* place."

The passionate outpouring from his wife's lips stunned Sean. Ann, like her father, Humphrey, was a peace-maker.

Damn Augusta for upsetting her.

"I try not to let her get to me, Sean. I really do. She's my mother. But she's getting worse. She has *always* tended to be overbearing, but she was never as bad as recently."

"Why didn't you say something, Annie? Before she reduced you and the girls to tears."

"She's my mother," Ann repeated. "I thought it was just a phase, and she'd get over it. I didn't want to make trouble."

And Sean knew. *She didn't say anything because she was afraid I'd lose my temper and make it even worse.*

Guilt turned his voice gruff.

"Still, you should have said. I could have talked to your father, and ..."

"And if he ever plucked up the courage to say anything, Mama would have made *his* life a misery. I couldn't."

"I understand." Sean kissed her forehead, answered by a sniffle as tears threatened to renew their flow.

And, he thought with a pang, *I do. I do understand. My Annie always puts others first.*

"Anyway." Ann had herself in hand again. "Today was the worst of all. I didn't feel well. I haven't for a while. I get so tense, Sean, waiting for her to come marching up the path, thumping that stick of hers on the porch, making demands before she's even decently inside. I just can't settle. The girls are almost as bad as me. I try to find tasks to keep them out of her way, but it's not always possible."

Sean nodded, deciding to keep his questions till she'd finished.

"So. Today. She didn't arrive till mid-afternoon. Some meeting or other she had to go to in the morning. I'd thought we were having a day free of her presence and the girls and I were having such a lovely time. We had the best china out for a little tea-party when Mama arrived, upsetting all our plans. She went on and on at Mary, the way she does."

Sean nodded while Ann continued without a pause.

"Mary's pinafore was soiled. She didn't wash her hands well enough. She set the table wrong. I tried to divert her attention, Sean, only this time it didn't work."

Sean nodded again, giving Ann a gentle hug.

"Poor Mary was so upset she spilt her cup of tea. Well it was milk, really, with just a spot of tea, you know. Mama shouted at her again, for being so clumsy and Mary jumped in tears, intent on running away. She bumped the table and knocked her cup onto the floor and broke the handle."

Ann shuddered, reliving that awful moment.

"Mama jumped up and slapped Mary across the face."

So, that's what caused the bruise. Sean's blood was fairly boiling by now, but Ann wasn't finished her tale of woe.

"She went too far, Sean. You or I might give them a tap on the bottom, but no-one else touches my babies. And to slap her face! And so hard! Mary screamed, poor love. Judy was so frightened, she screamed, too. Mama was yelling at all of us. Shadow was barking and barking, and, Sean, I'm so ashamed." This time Ann couldn't hold the tears back, and she sobbed in her husband's arms for several minutes before she wiped her eyes and concluded her recounting of events.

"I slapped Mama's face, Sean. I'm just as bad as she is. I slapped her across the face and dragged her out the door and yelled at her to go away and never come back. I yelled that I hated her. That I never wanted to see her again. Not ever. And I meant it. If she comes back, I'll bolt the door. I'm as bad as she is, Sean. I've inherited her nasty disposition. I can't stand myself."

In a rage, Sean wanted nothing more than to go tearing across the paddock and take Augusta Jackson by the throat and shake her until …

But Ann, sobbing and clinging to his arm, held him back until sanity returned. He'd deal with Augusta, right enough, but when he could be sure he wouldn't lose control. Coldly. That was the way to handle that termagant. He wouldn't give her the satisfaction of knowing she'd overset him. In the meantime, … His girls needed him. Especially his Ann.

"Come, darling. Shush. You're not one little bit like her. You were a mama tiger protecting her cubs, and you were so brave."

Still talking soothing nothings, he calmed Ann and led her inside where he noticed the debris of the tea-party, the broken cup still lying on the floor under the table and Mary's overturned chair next to it.

"What you need, Annie darling, is a nice long soak in the tub. I'll fix it for you, with some of your special lavender oil. Then the girls and I will clear up out here."

"But," Ann cast a sidelong glance towards the annexe, thinking longingly of immersing herself in hot, scented water. "I need to make dinner. You'll be hungry."

"Eggs on toast will do just fine, and I can fix them, Annie darling. The girls will help, won't you my sweets? Off you go. No arguments, now."

*****

The kitchen tidy again, Sean held the handle-less cup in his hand, turning it round and round.

"I'm sorry, Papa." Mary stood, hands behind her back, eyes abjectly turned towards the floor, waiting for him to mete out her punishment.

As if the poor mite hasn't been punished enough.

Sean crouched down in front of his daughter, a gentle finger lifting her chin so she could see he was smiling.

"I know how to cheer Mama for the loss of her cup."

He whispered in her ear, loving the sound of the little gurgle of laughter his suggestion elicited.

"C'mon, Judy. You can help." Hand in hand, the two girls ran into the garden.

Shortly after, they were back, clutching a fat pink rosebud and a fistful of daisies which their father helped them arrange in the broken cup.

"There now, my loves. We'll set this up here on the windowsill and turn it so you can't see it's broken. Think Mama will like it?"

Happy smiles and nods assured him his two youngest girls were already bouncing back.

Sean feared his Ann would take rather longer.

*****

"I'm just stepping out for a few minutes, my darling. No need to worry, I won't do anything rash."

The girls were tucked up and asleep, and Sean poured a cup of chamomile tea for Ann, then slapped his hat on his head and left, quietly closing the door behind him.

He hadn't liked the doubt darkening Ann's deep, brown eyes, so he'd be doubly sure to keep his temper on a tight rein.

Five minutes later he knocked on the door of the main house, waiting impatiently till Humphrey opened it.

"Humphrey, I'll apologise in advance, but I've got something to say to Augusta, and it won't keep."

Upright as if she had a poker down her back, Augusta sat enthroned in her sitting room, embroidery in her lap and Shadow curled up by her feet. Ignoring the dog's challenging half-growl, Sean halted at parade rest in front of her, doffing his hat. Humphrey, shuffling from foot to foot, hovered in the doorway behind him.

"I imagine you know why I'm here, Augusta. You overstepped the mark this afternoon. Badly. You've been upsetting my wife far too often recently, and it has to stop. Will stop."

"How dare you, " Augusta interrupted, but Sean cut through her bluster before she got into her stride.

"I dare, because I'll not have you upsetting my wife. Because I'll not have you striking my daughter on the face. I don't know your problem, Augusta, but you'll not take out your ill-temper on my family. Ann told you to stay away. I'm telling you too. Stay away from us. If Ann changes her mind, she will tell you. In the meantime, you are not welcome in our home. Good night Augusta."

Still in control of his temper by the slenderest of margins, Sean jammed his hat back on his head, turned smartly, and walked, seemingly calm and collected, out the door. Humphrey trotted like a terrier at his heels.

Outside in the blessed cool of the evening, Sean explained to his father-in-law what had happened.

"Sorry to drop you in the middle, Humphrey, but with me, Ann and the girls come first, and Ann's at the end of her tether. I'll be packing them up tomorrow and taking them away on a little holiday for a week or two. Until Ann feels up to coming home."

He'd only just thought of this, but the more he thought of it, the more it seemed the right thing to do.

Humphrey agreed.

"Probably the best thing for all of you, Sean, my boy. Ann's right. Augusta *is* getting worse. I've been hiding my head in the sand, but no longer. I'll have a word with Dr Samuels while you're away. Hopefully, he'll know what to do about her. Maybe there's something she can take to sweeten her moods."

5

The goldfields, 1888.

Southern Cross at last!

Throwing her hat in the air, Eliza cheered the end of their journey.

Then she looked around her, sobering quickly. She crept closer to Jason's side, clutching his hand. What was this place?

Their destination looked nothing like the country town of her imaginings.

It wasn't really a proper town at all. At least, not any sort of town she was familiar with. Many of the buildings were mere shacks. Unappealing ramshackle hovels, hastily thrown up from whatever flimsy materials came to hand.

Putting her hands up to shield her ears from the deafening clamour, Eliza had to step aside smartly to avoid being trampled by a trio of wild, roughly dressed miners rushing headlong down the street as they went about their business.

Choking dust caught in her throat, making her cough. She shrank back as a drunken miner, his arm round an equally drunk, scandalously clad woman, reeled past her, a bottle of rum clutched in his other hand. Early as it was, the hotels were doing a roaring trade.

Had it been possible, Eliza would have turned tail and ran. All two hundred and thirty miles back to the civilised streets of Perth.

"It's all right love," Jason whispered, taking her hand. "We won't be stayin' 'ere in town, ye know. George says we'll pick up our minin' permits and head out ta the goldfields in the mornin'." Head high, he eagerly surveyed his surroundings, not in the least put off by all that disgusted and terrified Eliza.

Heart sinking, Eliza saw his excitement. His eagerness to begin digging for his fortune. And although they'd reached Southern Cross, apparently this rough, frontier town wasn't even where the gold was!

"More walking!" Eliza protested.

"Jason, we've been walking forever already. How much further this time? Just so I know." She was sorry to sound so petulant, but this rowdy place scared her. Just when she thought she'd come to terms with her fears, too.

"About eight miles, George thinks. Then we'll pick our spot, stake our claim, and start diggin'. No more walkin' then, Eliza darlin'. I promise. We'll be ridin' in a carriage when we head back ta Perth."

Jason raised his hand, tucking a stray golden curl under her hat, his eyes caressing her lips.

If they'd been alone, he would have kissed her, but he had no intention of exposing his beautiful, innocent young wife to the attention of the wild looking men lounging around in the street. He shouldn't have brought his Eliza to this dangerous outpost where gold lured men of the worst kind, stripped of the thin veneer of civilisation. It was too late now, but Jason vowed to watch out for her.

No more walking after tomorrow!

Eliza felt like cheering again, but was too cowed and weary. If that carriage ride home was a promise, she'd hold Jason to it when the time came to return to the west coast. She smiled mistily up at her husband, reaching out to give his hand a reassuring squeeze. She could do this. She had to. She had no choice, so she'd make the best of it she could.

Actually, Eliza realised, the journey hadn't been all bad. Once she'd got in the way of the walking, she'd been able to look about her at the strange trees with their masses of unusual, yet beautiful flowers.

And the birds! So many, and so brightly coloured. She never tired of watching them. George had proved to be a fount of knowledge regarding the native flora and fauna with the result that this land no longer felt so dreadfully alien to her.

Sometimes, in the misty early mornings, she glimpsed true beauty in the landscape.

George had also taught both herself and Jason to set traps for the delightfully amusing small kangaroos the locals called wallabies. They were such good eating, although it still gave her nasty qualms to kill the pretty, gentle creatures.

She supposed it wasn't really any different to preparing the other meats she was accustomed to, chickens and lamb and beef, only she had never had to witness the process before. Never had to kill the animals herself, or watch the life die out in their eyes. Still, she always made sure to thank the Good Lord for His bounty, positive the addition of this fresh meat to their otherwise bland, stodgy diet had been responsible for their good health and stamina. She made a mental note to find out more about native foods if the opportunity should arise.

*****

"Righto Jason. Eliza. Up you get."

With the scent of gold in the air, George wasn't prepared to waste the day. At first light the next morning, with the cart restocked with foodstuffs, and miners' permits carefully stowed in their wallets, he urged them onto the road on the final leg of their journey, their destination was the aptly named Golden Valley, the site of the gold discoveries. Although the shopkeeper had been quick to inform Eliza it was named for a flower, the golden wattle, which turned the small valley into a blaze of bright yellow every Spring, and not for the gold being dug from the ground.

"Just ye wait a few months, missus. A real picture, it is," he'd assured her. "Smells pretty too."

"But it's already Spring," Eliza had answered, to be met with good-natured laughter.

"Nah, missus. This 'ere's Australia. The seasons are all turned around 'ere down under. This is Autumn. Hope ye packed warm coats, ye'll be needin' 'em soon. The wind whippin' across the flats gets pretty chilly."

It all sounded confusing to someone whose thinking was still based on English seasons, but Eliza was sure she would soon become accustomed to the differences. This unfamiliar land was her new home.

Unless they found enough gold to become fabulously wealthy, there was no way they would ever be returning to England, so it was a good thing she had already learned to like Australia.

*****

George Sampson, with Jason trailing at his heels, spent the whole afternoon poking around examining rocks and talking to miners who had already established their claims before he chose a site for them.

"See, they've found gold there, and there and over there," he explained, pointing out the successful claims.

"I reckon there's a vein running through and we'll be right on top of it. This low down in the valley we shouldn't have to go too deep, either. With two adjoining claims we'll be giving ourselves the best possible chance, so get those pegs hammered in, Jason lad, then we can get them registered and be back before dark."

While they were gone, Eliza puttered around the camp they had built on one corner of their joined claims.

This time, settling in for at least several months, they had taken far more trouble with their camp than was necessary for brief overnight shelter, unpacking and storing all their possessions under cover.

By the time the men returned, with full water barrels and a cart load of firewood gathered along the way, Eliza had built a fire and had a meal ready to serve.

With large rounds of tree trunks, uncut firewood really, for seats, and crates of tinned goods covered in a scrap of oilcloth for a table, and everything neatly ordered, their camp looked almost civilised.

"By Jove, Eliza girl. You've been busy and no mistake. You've made this place into a home already, that you have."

George flung down a roll of canvas he'd been carrying over his shoulder.

"I scrounged this for ye to make a shade here between the two sleeping tents. Sorta like a kitchen space. Thought ye deserved something a bit more comfortable. Soon as it's light, Jason and I will fix it up."

"George is right, Eliza. Ye've not complained at all over what we put ye through. I've been lookin' at what others have done, and soon ye'll have the snazziest home in the valley."

The snazziest home in the valley! A couple of tents, and makeshift furnishings under a canvas shadecloth! And Jason calls it snazzy.

Eliza felt like crying, but she had been looking too, and knew he was right. Compared to others they truly were well off. Blinking back the tears which had gathered unbidden in the corners of her eyes, she summoned up yet another smile.

"Thank you. Both of you. I've got some news too," she cheerfully informed them. "I was chatting with Hannah Glossup who lives on the claim two over."

Eliza turned and pointed to the rough bark shanty on the Glossup claim.

"Hannah told me there's a shop just over the hill a short way. Yesterday, the shopkeeper's assistant ran off to look for gold, so I'm heading over there tomorrow, bright and early, to ask for a job. That's what I used to do, George. I worked in a shop selling household goods and foodstuffs. When you say your prayers tonight, add one for me."

"There's no need for ye ta get a job, darlin". Ye've got me ta take care of ye." Jason's jaw set at a stubborn tilt, and Eliza steeled herself for an argument she was determined to win.

"It won't take me all day to keep this tiny space tidy, and you don't need me to help dig. I've seen how narrow the shafts are, and the two of you won't need me. If I can get a job, it will give me something to occupy my days. The money won't go astray either. Even if George is right about there being a vein of gold running underneath us, you've got to find it first, before our mine will begin paying out."

"But there's no need, love. I don't like the idea of ye tiring yerself out workin' in some shop. It won't be as nice as the one back home."

"I understand Jason." Eliza smiled and patted his hand, grateful he seemed to be coming round to the idea. "I've seen the makeshift shanties out here, but a shop's a shop, anywhere. The work will be similar."

Clasping his hand between both of hers, Eliza leaned forwards as she pleaded with Jason. "Please, I want to help. Let me do it my way."

Seeing her husband weakening, she produced her last argument.

"You know it was always my intention to work while we got ourselves set up here in our new country. If it's not satisfactory, I'll give it up. I promise."

Suddenly Eliza laughed. Standing up to collect the dirty tin plates, she flashed a cheeky grin.

"Jason darling, why are we bickering over this? I have to get the job first."

"Yeah, ye do. Just promise ta forget the idea if the bloke in the shop isn't the sort ta treat a woman right." Eliza nodded, happy to leave it at that.

*****

"Good morning Mr Jones."

Eliza thrust her hand out to the large, apron-clad bald man swiping a grubby cloth over the two planks balanced on trestles which did rough duty as a counter. Suspiciously studying Eliza from beneath louring brows, he extended a meaty paw, engulfing his neatly dressed visitor's small, gloved hand.

"My name is Eliza Baker, Mr Jones. Mrs Jason Baker. I arrived here recently with my husband, Jason Baker, and his partner, Mr George Sampson. I'm hoping you and I can be of use to each other, Mr Jones."

Eliza gave the shopkeeper one of the persuasive smiles she had used on the more affluent customers in the English shop she had worked in from leaving school till she married Jason and set out for Australia.

"And what kind of use do you reckon on us being to each other Mrs Baker?"

Sam Jones tossed his duster into a box under the counter, slapped the dust from his hands, and leaned brawny forearms on the clean patch.

Eliza swallowed, marshalling her carefully rehearsed persuasions.

"I'm hoping to find employment in your shop, Mr Jones. Before leaving England several months ago I worked for quite a few years in an establishment similar in kind to yours. The building was rather more permanent," smiling to show she meant no offence, she cast a critical eye over Mr Jones' premises, mentally cataloguing the merchandise, "but we sold roughly the same types of goods. I'm quite proficient at shop work. I can weigh and measure, add up accurately and handle money competently. I am scrupulously honest. Indeed, my previous employer trusted me to mind the shop alone anytime he had to go out for an hour or two."

There had been no appreciable change in Mr Jones' stony expression, but Eliza could see he was listening intently to her every word, so she ploughed doggedly on.

"Of course, you only have my word for it that I'm telling you the truth, Mr Jones, but I assure you I am."

Eliza ground to a halt. Uncertain what to do next, she simply clasped her hands loosely and waited.

The man in front of her heaved himself up to his full height and looked her over, taking in her clean, tidy appearance and the nervous clasping and unclasping of her hands.

Mrs Eliza Baker wasn't desperate as so many of the women he saw enter his shop were, and he found himself reluctantly impressed with her initiative.

"Here's what we'll do, young lady. I need an assistant I can trust to do the job honestly and efficiently. I've always had a man before, but the men round here are more interested in digging for gold than working for me. If you can satisfy me that you can do the job, then we'll have ourselves a deal."

A tired, gaunt woman with two small children hanging off her skirts edged round the open door. Sam Jones continued speaking to Eliza over his shoulder as he moved away to serve his customer.

"I'll give you half an hour to look around and familiarise yourself with my merchandise, prices and how I've got it all arranged. As you can see, all prices are clearly marked. I don't let anyone keep a tab. It's cash up front every time. No exceptions for hard luck stories. I'm running a business, not a charity. At the end of the half hour, I'll stand back awhile and watch how you manage the customers. By the way Mrs Baker, folks call me Sam, and I'd be obliged if you'd do the same."

Eliza beamed.

"You won't be disappointed Sam, and since we're going to be working together, I'd be honoured if you call me Eliza."

*****

The next two hours flew by, as Eliza settled into the rhythm of serving customers once again. By the time the morning rush eased off, Sam Jones knew he had a winner in Eliza. She'd been every bit as good as her word.

His gruff "You'll do, girlie," brought a proud glow to Eliza's cheeks.

It was nice to have one's efforts appreciated, especially when she'd worked so hard to impress. She wouldn't be earning much, but it would be enough to make a difference. Especially if the gold failed to eventuate as quickly as the men expected it to. If, indeed, it eventuated at all. Eliza couldn't wait to share her little triumph with Jason.

"Eliza," Sam said as she took off her apron and replaced it in her shopping bag, "Here's a little something for this morning."

He bundled up a bacon bone and a handful of the pitifully few vegetables remaining in their boxes, thrusting them into her hands.

"My sons are due in with a fresh load this afternoon. You may as well take these. They're not much, but you can make them into a pot of soup." Sam's gesture was a pleasant surprise since Eliza had assumed her morning's trial would be unpaid.

"Oh Sam, thanks ever so much."

Eliza was secretly amused by how her standards had changed. What she would once have thought paltry, she now viewed as genuine treasure. Sam could have sold what he had given her for more than her brief couple of hours work were worth, confirming what she had begun to suspect.

While watching him dealing with his customers, she twice caught him slipping a little extra to care-worn women with subdued, hungry looking children at their heels. It looked as if Sam Jones' bite might be considerably less than his bark. She smiled, preparing to leave, then turned back suddenly.

"By the way, Sam, do you mind if I put a notice up here in your shop tomorrow? George wants to sell his horse and cart, now that we're settled in. It's hard to find grazing for the poor animal, and he's going to be too busy digging to go looking far and wide for grass every day."

"No need for that, Eliza. Tell him to come and see me tonight. My boys were talking about expanding their freight service. They'll give him a fair price and take good care of the horse."

"I'll do that, Sam. See you bright and early tomorrow."

Eliza just barely kept her feet to a decorous walk on the way home, but there was no way she could wipe the beaming smile off her face. Now all that was needed was for the men to find gold, and life would be near perfect.

Maybe now she would stop having those tiresome dreams, nightmares really, that had begun disturbing her sleep. She never remembered them clearly when she woke, sweating and gasping for breath, but the feeling of dread they left in their wake was making her grouchy in the mornings.

6

Perth & New Norcia, May, 1888

Cold winds with the possibility of intermittent showers were predicted for later in the week, but for the first three days of the O'Grady's holiday, the sun shone warmly out of a clear, blue sky. The boarding house overlooking the Swan River was comfortable, and long, rambling walks along the river, building sandcastles at the water's edge, and the discovery of a nearby tea-shop where they could buy the rich, cream-filled cakes the girls loved, were all working the magic Sean had hoped for. Just this morning he'd heard Ann laugh for the first time since the upheaval.

The farm would be in good hands with the men Humphrey employed, all of whom Sean had chosen himself, so, when Humphrey had told him to take as long as needed, he decided to take his father-in-law at his word. Ann deserved a good long break.

He'd see she had it.

"Sean?" his wife's diffident enquiry broke into his thoughts, and he turned to her with a reassuring smile.

"There's something I've been thinking about. Thinking hard."

Ann checked that the girls were happily occupied out of earshot before continuing.

"I want to leave. Go somewhere new. Where it's just us. Where Mama can't come barging through the door any time she wants." She looked up, a plea darkening her eyes. "The way she is these days, Mama's bad for Mary and Judith. Bad for me, too."

"I agree, Annie love. But moving away is a bit drastic, isn't it? Do you really believe that's necessary? Your father will miss you. What if Dr Samuels is able to restore your mother?"

"Restore her to what? She's always been difficult, Sean. I know Papa will miss us, but it can't be helped. Sean darling, there's going to be another baby, before the end of the year, and I simply can't cope if Mama's there, telling me what I'm doing wrong all the time. I've got to get away, Sean! I've got to, or I'll go crazy!"

"Another baby! Annie, are you sure? That's wonderful news, the very best, but are you sure?"

"Course I'm sure, silly."

Sean whooped for joy, kissed his wife and made all the proper exclamations and comments, but underneath, Ann's desire to escape was turning over and over in his mind. The surge of sheer relief it sent through him felt as if a huge weight he didn't know he carried was being lifted from his shoulders. When Ann returned to the subject of moving, he was ready to discuss ways and means.

"Seriously, Annie. Where would you like to live?"

"You're a farmer, Sean. Can we afford to buy a farm of our own? Perhaps Papa could help …"

"No need to go to your father, darling. You remember that legacy last year, from my uncle?"

Ann laughed.

"The legacy from the uncle who struck it rich at Ballarat?" She'd always thought the story something of a fairy tale, much exaggerated to entertain the children. An idea her husband had never disabused her of.

Sean nodded.

"The very one. You never did ask how much he left me, just if there was enough for new dresses. Which there was."

A sly smile twitching his lips, he waited for her to ask. The legacy was a substantial nest-egg he'd put aside for a rainy day. After buying the new dresses of course. Ann may have laughed the legacy off, but in truth he could more than afford a farm of his own, and would have bought one at the time, except for not wanting to let Humphrey down. Added to that, he was thrifty with his wages. Ann would have more household help than a washerwoman in future, wherever they lived.

"Then I'd better rectify that omission, darling," she laughed. "Are we rich? Rich enough to buy our own farm away from here?"

Leaning close, Sean whispered the total at the bottom of his last bank statement, loving the way Ann's eyes widened and her mouth opened, awestruck.

"Then there's nothing holding us back?" She laughed aloud, the care and worry falling away leaving her as bright-eyed and happy as she had on their wedding day.

"Let's do it, Sean. Right now. Today. I don't want to waste a minute."

Her enthusiasm infecting him, too, Sean laughed with her. Jumping to his feet, he hauled her up then leaned down to pick up the rug and picnic basket.

"Mary! Judith! Your Mama wants to go shopping."

"What are we going to buy, Mama? Can I have the book about kittens we saw yesterday?"

"Can I have a new dolly?"

"Darlings, a book about kittens and a new dolly are top of the list, but first we're going to buy Papa a new farm of his very own. Won't that be exciting?"

*****

Books and dolls were easily procured. A farm took a while longer, but several days after they'd spoken to a land broker, he sent them a note advising of a property meeting their specifications which had just come on the market.

Mrs Botham, an elderly widow from the lay community adjoining the monastery lands at New Norcia was selling up following her husband's death.

"Look, here it is."

Pouring over the map in Mr Protheroe's office, Sean pointed out the farm, *Wattle Bend*.

"It's on a bend in the creek."

"A guaranteed year-round supply of good water, Mr O'Grady," interjected Mr Protheroe.

"And see how close it is to the Monastery, Sean. There looks to be a proper village. What shops are there, Mr Protheroe? How many neighbours are there? What's the house like?"

Sean laughed as Ann's eager, rapid-fire questions poured out.

"More to the point, Mr Protheroe," he interjected, "how many acres are under plough? And what stock is there? Wherever we buy, we have to make a decent living."

Taking their questions one by one, Mr Protheroe returned a stream of positive answers.

"You'll notice, Mr O'Grady," he pointed out, "The monks operate a flour mill and there is a police station in addition to the other facilities Mrs O'Grady asked about."

"And, Sean," Ann whispered, "did you see on the map? New Norcia is almost a hundred miles from Papa's farm on the Upper Swan River. Too far for Mama to bother me except by letters, but not too far for visits when we *want* to see them. It sounds ideal."

It did sound good, but Sean wasn't going to be rushed into buying a pig in a poke. This was his family's future at stake. They'd go about this the right way.

"If this *Wattle Bend* farm is all you claim it to be, Mr Protheroe, then you'll have made a sale, but I'll be taking a trip to New Norcia to see it for myself, first."

"Which is exactly what I would advise, Mr O'Grady."

*****

"If you think you're leaving me behind, Sean O'Grady, think again." Hands on hips, Ann argued the point. "It will be my home, too, you know, and it was my idea into the bargain. We'll go to inspect *Wattle Bend* together."

They each had more to say on the subject, before Sean agreed, but when they closed their bedroom door that evening after tucking the girls in, they were in perfect accord. They were still in perfect accord the next morning, Ann's cheeks warming to a rosy pink when Sean took advantage of helping her into the carriage to caress the delightfully feminine curve of her bottom.

"Come on girls," he called, not bothering to hide his grin, "up beside your mother, now. We're off on an adventure."

A week later Sean signed on the dotted line, and a week after that, he swept his wife up in his arms, carrying her across the threshold of their new home. The lawyers were still shuffling paper, but old Mrs Botham was as eager to go to her daughter's as they were to take possession.

"We're home, my darling. Home and safe."

7

The goldfields, 1888.

"Oh, Sam," Eliza confided as she tied her apron strings and took her place behind the counter. "Nine more tents went up since yesterday in our sector alone. Every day I count more and yet more tents filling the valley."

"I've been counting, too, Eliza. It's good for business, of course," he shrugged. "I've sent instructions to my boys to bring us as much stock as they can rustle up."

"Yes, but Sam? Where's it going to end? They can't all strike it rich, can they? What will happen to those who don't find gold?"

She was thinking of her own two men, still hopeful, but yet to see that magical shimmer of gold in the light of their candles. *What will happen to us?* was the real question she asked Sam.

Sam Jones, well aware of Eliza's situation, stroked his chin, considering his answer carefully.

He didn't want to upset her, but the truth was, every day saw some man driven to the edge of despair when his luck failed him and his wife and children, barefoot and ragged, stared hopelessly at the world from hollow-eyed, hungry faces. Steady traffic now flowed in both directions on the road between Southern Cross and Perth, although the majority of travellers were still eager new arrivals.

"Lady Luck is a very fickle mistress, my dear," he temporised. "The sensible ones will know when to turn their back on her and seek their fortunes elsewhere. The others ..." he shrugged again. "They never learn. Once the gold-lust gets a tight grip on a man, he'll follow its lure to the death."

Eliza shivered, wondering just how far gone Jason was. Could he still turn his back on the gold? Still make the good life they'd planned together?

Sam's mention of death had struck at Eliza's heart. She'd seen for herself that worse fates existed than merely failing to discover the elusive gold. Men were crippled or killed when shafts and tunnels collapsed, or ropes snapped. Eliza felt a sickening dread each time the shout went up; followed by an equally sickening relief when she discovered it was some other woman's husband who had become a sacrificial victim to the Golden Goddess.

Winter settled over the land. Bitterly cold winds combined with inadequate shelter and poor nutrition meant sickness became rife. To make matters worse, winter was the rainy season. With only flimsy canvas walls to protect them from the wet, everything became damp and clammy. Cooking fires smoked, stinging eyes, and clothes didn't dry properly.

Eliza was more grateful than ever for her job in Sam Jones's General Store. At least she and her two men were better fed and more adequately clothed than most, and therefore more resistant to the plethora of coughs, agues and fevers. Still, even in the midst of such discomfort there were moments of pure joy to lighten their hearts.

Like the day Hannah Glossup who lived two claims over with her husband and three sons gave birth to a tiny baby girl. Nearly every woman on the field appeared at Hannah's door, many with a gift of food or baby clothes in hand, all wishing baby Aurea, her daddy's golden haired darling, good fortune.

"Oh Jason," Eliza sighed, stitching away at a baby blanket fashioned from a yard of pink flannel purchased from the store. "Little Aurea is the most perfect wee thing you could ever see."

"Here, I say Eliza, ye not goin' clucky on me, are ye?"

Jason's question was meant to be a joke, and Eliza laughed dutifully, denying any such thing, but underneath his jocular words she detected a tinge of panic. Although the mere thought of a baby of her own aroused gut-wrenching fear in Eliza, she couldn't help wondering if her husband's fears arose from the same source as her own.

During the first months of her marriage Eliza had been disappointed not to fall pregnant. Now, after seeing how easily babies and young children sickened and died as a result of the dreadful conditions prevailing on the goldfields, she considered her barren state a blessing.

Not that she didn't want children. She did. More than anything else, she longed to hold Jason's baby to her breast.

Only not in this awful place. Some nights the longing for a home of her own, a proper home with solid walls and roof, was so strong she cried herself to sleep.

Her fears were given new strength when Baby Aurea succumbed to croup a few short weeks later, the pink blanket stitched with so much love and hope becoming her shroud.

Eliza took care to shed her tears where neither of her men could see.

Shortly after, Tom Glossup abandoned his unproductive claim and took his family back to Albany where they had come from. Too late, however, to save Aurea's life, or Hannah's broken heart. Eliza shed tears of her own on saying farewell to her first, and best, friend on the diggings.

The rain blowing up from the frigid Southern Ocean, turned the bare dust to mud.

From complaining about the invasive dust, the women now cursed the quagmire underfoot. The damp clothes and bedding exacerbated the illnesses, and, above all other woes stood the grossly inflated cost of everything they needed for survival.

Every single item needed had to be hauled in at great expense by enterprising opportunists like the Jones boys, to be sold at an exorbitant profit. The miners produced nothing to support themselves.

"How was your day, darling?" Eliza turned from the stew she stirred over the fire, smoky from damp wood, to greet her husband. Resting her hands on his shoulders to hold herself away from his dirt, she leaned forward to kiss him on the lips.

"Umm. All the better for this. Thank God I've got you, Lizzie darling, or this place would send me right round the twist. I swear, if we still had Hercules, I could make more money haulin' supplies than I'm getting' from the ground. Even farmin' would be a more productive reason fer diggin'."

Eliza's heart soared, thinking her husband might be ready to toss it in and walk away. About to encourage him to do just that, she was interrupted by the arrival of George and another neighbour, Charlie McManus.

"Hey Jason, have you heard?" Lips tightening, Eliza turned back to her stew-pot. Only one kind of news aroused excitement like Charlie's, an assumption proved by his very next words.

"Like I was just tellin' old George, here, Frenchie just happened on the vein of gold we're all lookin' for. And that's good news for us and all, as it's pointin' right in our direction. I reckon you two will make a strike any day now, and then me. I'm gunna start a new shaft, more in line with Frenchie's."

"Charlie's in the right of it, Jason, lad. We've just got to hold in there a bit longer, then we'll be made." George looked over his shoulder, including Eliza in the conversation. "Did you hear that, Eliza. Soon be our turn. But don't you think I don't appreciate what you do for us, 'cause I do. Your job makes all the difference. Why, I reckon we'd have had to throw in the towel without you keepin' us all fed."

How's that for irony.

Hiding her true thoughts behind her smile, Eliza continued stirring, hoping Charlie didn't plan on cadging a meal. A small pot of stew only went so far, and she already had two hungry men to feed besides herself.

"Ye're a lifesaver, right enough, Lizzie darlin'," Jason murmured in her ear, "but I still wish we didn't have ta rely on ye the way we do. It's not fittin' for a man ta be kept by his wife."

"Sounds as if it won't be for much longer, Jason," she murmured back, not believing a word of it, "then you can keep me in comfort for the rest of our lives."

Well, what else could I say? Complaining will get me nowhere. Yet. But one day soon, Eliza vowed, she'd take a stand. When she was sure of winning.

Eagerly counting the days till Jason finally admitted defeat and took her somewhere they could start what she considered their real life in Australia, Eliza began making new plans. For her this period on the diggings was merely a phase they were passing through. A phase which she judged to be almost over.

The sun strengthened with the change of season and Eliza's lilting voice was frequently raised in song as she went about the drudgery of her daily tasks. Believing their time was nearly up, for the first time since her arrival on the goldfields she felt truly happy.

Until her dreams were shattered. By success, of all things.

"Eliza! Eliza, we've done it at last. We've struck gold."

Jason came running to meet her on her way home from work, catching her up in his arms and dancing her round and round in the middle of the road.

"Come and see, love. It's so shiny and pretty. Just like ... Like gold, Lizzie."

Jason's goofy grin did little to lift Eliza's spirits from the depths into which they had plummeted at his words.

Just when Eliza thought she had experienced the worst the goldfields could throw at her; when she thought Jason was almost ready to give up and head back to Perth; they had to go and strike gold. It *was* exciting, she had to admit. And frustrating. Because, in spite of Jason's optimism it was not a lot of gold, which might have been of some use.

Just a thin little vein, a mere thread, glittering in the light of the lantern when Jason persuaded her to clamber down the shaft to see the mighty treasure they'd spent so many agonising months digging to find. The sight had her weeping her eyes out, scrambling to escape the claustrophobic tunnel at the bottom of their shaft.

She let the men believe her tears were of joy, but Eliza knew they really sprang from despair. Now, jubilant with hope restored, there'd be no dragging Jason away. Eliza resigned herself to being stuck in this awful place for more interminable months.

For several days Eliza pretended to have a cold to excuse her reddened eyes.

The trace of gold, for that was all it was, a trace, was enough to renew the men's enthusiasm. George was exultant, claiming his belief in their claim was vindicated, even when the tiny vein pinched out a couple of weeks later.

Winter gave way to a brief Spring, the few scraggy wattles that hadn't yet been turned into firewood, did their poor best to warrant the valley's name, although most newcomers thought Golden Valley was named for the gold under the ground, not nature's floral bounty.

Eliza clambered to the top of the hill to pick a bunch of the fragrant fluffy balls, only to be disappointed when they shrivelled up by the next day.

8

New Norcia, November, 1888.

"What answer will you give your father?"

In her veritable cascade of letters to her daughter, Augusta had been begging to be allowed to visit. Today Humphrey had written a letter of his own, supporting his wife's expressed wishes.

The book he'd been reading in bed cast aside, Sean lay propped on his elbow alongside Ann, his hand on her bulging tummy, feeling their baby vigorously exercising her limbs.

Of course, she might be he.

Which was what Ann maintained, claiming this pregnancy felt different, and must, therefore, be a boy.

Which will be nice, Sean thought, paying more attention to his wife's body than their conversation, *but as long as mother and child are healthy, I'll be happy with another beautiful daughter.*

Ann eased herself into a sitting position, and Sean, raising himself to sit at her side, slipped an extra pillow behind her back.

"Oh, darling. I really do want to see Papa again. I miss him so much. Mary and Judy do, too. I was thinking, it's Mary's birthday in two weeks. We could ask them to come for a week or two and see how it goes."

"Humphrey says the tablets Dr Samuels prescribed are doing wonders, and your mother is much improved."

"Yes." Ann sounded less than sure, but she couldn't shut her mother out of her life forever. Didn't really want to. Augusta hadn't always been the tartar she had become.

"I'll tell them to come in time for Mary's special day, then if the visit is not going well, I'll blame Baby." She patted her tummy apologetically. "I'll say I'm too tired for a longer visit, and cut their stay short. If I tell them they can come back for Baby's christening at New Year, I know Papa will understand."

"If you're sure. With Joan and Polly to help, you won't have to lift a finger, you know."

"They're so good, Sean, only I can't help wondering what Mama will think of native servants. She's always refused to employ any."

"Well, as to that, with their husbands working in the fields with me, we'd be silly to hire a white woman to replace Joan and Polly. Unless that's what you'd prefer?"

"No. Of course not. I like them. They've become friends as well as servants. Mama can just get used to them," Ann declared.

"They do an excellent job, then go home to their own houses at night, leaving us to our own company. It's an arrangement which suits me very well, my darling. I'll write to Mama and Papa tomorrow."

*****

Ann barely had time to prepare the guest room after receiving her parents' acceptance before their carriage bowled up to the front door.

"Ann. Oh, Daughter, I've missed you so much." Augusta hadn't waited to be helped, scrambling down to envelop Ann in her embrace.

"But, … You're so big!" Her hand on Ann's greatly expanded waistline indicated her meaning. Augusta's face dropped. Drawing back abruptly, hurt and accusation together turning her lips into a familiar hard, angry line, she exploded.

"When you told us about the baby last month, I took it to mean you'd only just started. You kept it secret from me, your own mother! How could you be so cruel?" Tears sprang into her eyes, making Ann feel guilty.

"Now, now, Augusta dear," Humphrey murmured. "You know Dr Samuels said you were not to upset yourself."

Ann took inspiration from her father's words.

"That's right, Mama. When Dr Samuels said you were not to have any excitement, I thought it best to wait. You have Sean to thank, you know, that I told you when I did. He claimed the doctor only meant unpleasant excitement. Sean said good news never hurt anyone."

Her husband had said so, but the main reason Ann had held back was to save herself from having her mother descend upon her before *she* was ready.

"And where is my favourite son-in-law? And my granddaughters?" Humphrey gave his daughter a hug and a kiss.

"We weren't expecting you till tomorrow, Papa, so Sean took the girls down the paddock to see some new lambs. They'll be back soon. But why are we standing outside in the heat. Come in and let me show you my home."

The house at *Wattle Bend* was far more spacious than the manager's cottage on the Jackson farm. Even so, the tour took no more than a minute or two, and Ann, removing Shadow, her mother's pug, to the verandah, left her parents to freshen up after their journey.

"Come to the sitting room when you're ready, Mama. Papa. I'll have Joan make a pot of tea."

Ann set the tray herself to be sure it met her mother's exacting standards, handed Joan a clean apron, and was sitting primly in her favourite armchair when her parents returned.

Augusta stared hard at Joan when she brought in the tea-tray, but Ann's housekeeper had been well-trained, keeping her eyes down and bobbing a half-curtsey.

"Well," Augusta gave the tray a close scrutiny. "This all looks very nice, but tell me, Ann. How do you find these *black* servants?" Mortified to hear her mother use such a derogatory tone in front of Joan, Ann bit her tongue. This was not the time to provoke an argument.

"I'd have thought you would be more comfortable with someone like my Mrs Brearley," Augusta continued.

And so the conversation went on. Augusta still acerbic and critical as usual, but now not unduly so. On tenterhooks for the first hour, Ann had relaxed by the time Sean and the girls arrived home. Augusta, obviously on her best behaviour, only occasionally demonstrated the imperiousness her daughter had learned to expect. Ann had noticed Humphrey slip his wife a little blue pill which she washed down with her cup of tea, and correctly attributed her mildness to medical intervention.

If those pills keep Mama on a pleasant, even keel, she thought, *then I'm all for them.*

*****

The little blue pills continued to do their work. When the girls began a noisy chasing game with Shadow, which would previously have aroused her grandmother's considerable ire, it was met with no more than a severe frown.

"Oops. Sorry Mama," Mary, correctly interpreting her mother's urgent gesture, apologised prettily, taking her little sister and the dog outside. Ann breathed a silent sigh of relief at having averted what might have escalated into an unpleasant incident, so easily. Would have in the past.

On the day of the birthday party, with half a dozen assorted children invited to share afternoon tea, things grew a little rowdy and cracks began to appear in Augusta's composure. That day disaster was averted when Humphrey slipped her an extra pill and suggested she lie down in their room. Even Sean was the recipient of his mother-in-law's signature "Humph!" less frequently than previously.

Standing on the verandah with her father one afternoon towards the end of the visit, Ann slipped her arm around Humphrey's waist, resting her head against his shoulder while they watched Augusta throw a ball to Judith, teaching her to play catch.

"I'm so glad you and Mama came, Papa dear. I've enjoyed this visit so much. It's a real pleasure to see Mama so improved. She seems so much happier, too. What does Dr Samuels say?"

"As you know, he attributed her illness to the problems which are known to afflict some women when they reach a certain age." Humphrey ran a surreptitious finger around his collar, surprised to find it wasn't tight at all. "He thinks she'll grow out of it. In a few more months he wants to experiment with lessening her reliance on the tablets he prescribed. See how she goes on."

"Good news, surely, Papa?" Ann gave him a quick hug. "Ooh, I do feel tired. Don't take this the wrong way, Papa dear, but I'll be glad to wave you goodbye the day after tomorrow so I can sit back with my feet up and do nothing at all except wait to welcome Baby." A dreamy smile curved her lips as her hand rose to rest protectively upon her baby bulge.

Not long now, little one.

"Don't blame you one iota, Annie dear," Humphrey murmured, averting his eyes. "Even the most well-loved visitors can outstay their welcome. I think Augusta will be more settled now she can imagine you in this very pleasant home of yours. It's more in the nature of what she's always wanted for you."

"Will you come with us to the Maguire's tomorrow?"

Brian and Pauline Maguire, neighbours with young children for Mary and Judith to play with, had become firm friends with the O'Grady family, and Pauline Maguire had invited Ann and Augusta to tea before the Jacksons left for home the following day.

"I will. Otherwise I'll worry all afternoon. I don't think you should be taking the reins, and neither should your mother."

*****

Sean, on his way to join Bill and Tommy Smith, his Aboriginal farmhands, in the fields, waved off his wife, daughters and in-laws on their neighbourly visit. Blowing kisses, Mary and Judith leaned over the back of the buckboard until they passed out of sight. In less than half an hour Humphrey steered the horse through the gate in front of the Maguire's homestead. Jostling each other to be first, Mary and Judith scrambled down and ran to meet their friends, all the children disappearing out of sight around the corner of the house as Pauline Maguire emerged onto her verandah to welcome her guests.

"Pauline, hello. It's so good to see you." Ann called, standing and extending her hand to her father, waiting to help her down.

Shadow, who'd been dozing under Augusta's feet, woke with a startled yap, realising the children had gone without him. Lunging forward, he pulled his leash out of his mistress's hand, and leapt to the ground, intent on catching up with the children, whom he loved.

When questioned afterwards, no-one was quite sure how it had happened, but as Ann went to step down, Shadow's leash caught around her foot, tripping her up. Humphrey made a valiant effort to catch her as she fell, but she knocked him off his feet. Landing awkwardly, sprawled on the path beside her father, Ann's head lay at an unnatural angle against one of the white-painted rocks lining the Maguire's front path.

In the still afternoon air, Pauline Maguire always maintained she had heard the crack as Ann's neck snapped.

For one fraught moment, not so much as a bird uttered a single sound. And then pandemonium reigned.

"Ann! Ann! Answer me!"

"Mrs O'Grady! Oh, Mr Jackson! Whatever shall we do?"

Augusta, still in the carriage, began screaming. A high, wordless scream which raised the hair on the back of the neck of all who heard her and set their teeth on edge. A scream which went on and on, bringing servants and children running to add to the cacophony.

"She's gone, poor young lady."

Mrs Warner, the Maguire's housekeeper, pushed forward to kneel at Humphrey's side, taking charge of the situation.

"Leave her to me, sir," she commanded. "You take your wife inside and see to her, if you please. Mrs Maguire, Ma'am, this is no fit place for these children."

Riders were sent post-haste to fetch Sean and the Police Constable from New Norcia. The latter brought with him one of the monks skilled in medical matters, but of course they arrived too late to help Ann.

9

The goldfields, January – March, 1889.

Shortly before Christmas, Eliza, hot, dusty and tired, trudged home from work to find Jason, George, Charlie and a couple of others sharing a drink under her shadecloth.

"Eliza! Eliza darlin'! We done it! We found the main seam we were lookin' fer. We're diggin' up real gold, this time, Lizzie, not just a trace. A nice thick seam."

"He's right, Eliza," George added, waving a bottle of beer in her direction. "Put your best dress on, my dear. We're taking you down to Maisie Baddams's cookhouse for dinner tonight to celebrate."

Life in the mining camp all at once became easier, now they had money coming in and Eliza began dreaming once more of their return to civilisation.

*****

"Just imagine, Jason, we'll build a house of our own, with a bedroom and sitting room. We'll have comfortable furniture and decent clothes again. I'll have my little shop, selling clothes for women and children, I think. I've had enough of groceries. You'll be a respected carpenter, with people coming to you to build their houses. We'll live in a nice little town and go to church on Sunday, all dressed up in our Sunday best. Oh, darling, it will be wonderful. I'm so looking forward to our new life, aren't you?"

Rising onto her elbow, Eliza leaned over her husband, kissing him with a warmth which tiredness and anxiety had leached from her in recent months. She ran her fingers down his bare chest, her body heating in response to the fire she read in his eyes.

Wrapping a muscular arm around her waist, Jason crushed Eliza to his chest, returning her kisses with interest. With a breathless laugh, he flipped her over onto her back, beneath him.

That night they made love with the joyous abandon of the early months of their marriage, waking early to make love again before the kookaburras called them to rise and shine.

"Better than an alarm clock, those flammin' birds are," Jason grumbled, buttoning his rough work-shirt. Coming back to the bed where Eliza lay watching him, he took her hand in his, dropping a kiss into her palm.

"I love ye, Lizzie girl. Really, truly love ye. I've been thinkin' about what you were sayin' last night." He smoothed his thumb over the palm he'd kissed, choosing his next words carefully.

"What ye said about a house and your little dress shop and all. That's what ye really want, isn't it? Ye've been behind me a hundred percent, but a miner's life isn't fer ye, is it, love?"

Eliza shook her head.

"No it isn't, Jason darling," she admitted, "but you were right when you said we'd regret it if we didn't give it a try, and it looks as if it's going to work out just fine." She lifted the hand he wasn't holding, lying it against his cheek.

"I trust you, Jason, and I'll support you in your dream as long as you don't forget I have dreams, too. It doesn't have to be a shop. That's simply an idea. My *true* dream is of a home and family. The two of us, together with our children, if we're so blessed. Somewhere my head doesn't pound to the beat of the stamper. Where digging in the ground is to make a garden, with flowers to feed our souls and vegetables to feed our bodies. But it won't work unless you want it too, Jason."

"Oh, Lizzie, I do. I surely do. This minin' is no more ta my taste than yours, only … Can ye hang on a while longer? Till we put together a big enough nest egg to set us up? We'll go to the bank and open an account. I'll give ye every spare penny we make, fer ye to keep safe. Ye'll have yer dream home, Lizzie darlin', I promise," Jason said, solemnly sealing the promise with a kiss.

"Anyway, that's George I hear out there stokin' the fire ta make breakfast. Up ye get, Lizzie darlin'."

Eyes brimming with grateful tears, Eliza yelped as Jason playfully swatted her on the bottom, then laughed and clambered out of bed.

*****

Eliza opened her bank account as Jason suggested, but even though she managed to make a deposit each week, the amounts varied and the total grew too slowly to satisfy her impatience. Especially as her suspicion she was expecting a child became a certainty when February edged into March. Doing endless calculations in her head, she tried to estimate how long to wait before insisting she and Jason pack up and head west.

For the one thing Eliza was absolutely sure of was that she would not be having her baby on the goldfields.

It wasn't only the death of little Aurea Glossop which informed her it would be a bad idea. Every day, it seemed, she heard hair-raising tales of illnesses and epidemics in mining communities where insanitary conditions produced a horrifyingly high rate of infant mortality. Or maybe she'd been hearing such stories all along, and was only now taking them personally. Either way, her baby would not be born anywhere east of the tiny town of Northam.

June.

She would give Jason till June, she decided. Early July at the latest, and then they were leaving, regardless of the size of their nest-egg. Earlier still if the gold petered out again as it had last year. Eliza fingered the brooch Jason had given her for Christmas, and which she wore every day like a talisman. Made from their own gold, it was a heart, engraved with their entwined initials beneath the Southern Cross.

She loved it.

Loved the sentiment behind it, but if it meant the difference between safety or danger for her baby, she wouldn't hesitate to sell it.

Decision made, Eliza hurried the last few yards to work. Tonight, snuggled up in bed next to her husband, she'd tell him about the baby.

*****

"Sam! Sam," Charlie McManus, panting for breath, clutched at the stitch in his side.

"In a minute, Charlie. Can't you see I'm serving a customer?"

"I can't wait, Sam Jones. I need to speak to Eliza. Where is she?"

Sam and the women in his shop gaped at Charlie, only now taking in his wild-eyed desperation. Before they could ask the questions forming on their tongues, Eliza burst through the curtain separating the shop-front from the storeroom behind where she'd been unpacking fresh stock. Lips trembling, she grabbed hold of Charlie's arms, shaking him urgently.

"Charlie! What's wrong? Has something happened to Jason? Or George?" she added, for only something bad could account for Charlie McManus leaving his mine to speak to her in the middle of a busy morning.

"Oh, Eliza, girl. I'm that sorry to be the one ta tell ya."

"Tell me what?" Eliza fairly screamed the question.

Sam moved closer, putting a steadying arm around her shoulder.

His customers hung on Charlie's every word, storing up the tale to share with their neighbours. Bad news travelled fast, and drew a wide audience.

"It's Jason, Eliza. There was a rockfall in the shaft."

"Nooo!" Eliza's knees sagged, and for a moment the world went frighteningly dark.

"He's not dead, Lizzie. George and all of us got him out." Charlie gulped, hoping his words still held true. "He's hurt bad, though, Lizzie. George sent me ta fetch ya to his side."

Not waiting for more, Eliza tore off, dodging traffic as she raced headlong down the road back to their claim.

Back to Jason.

"Jason! Jason!"

Eliza thrust her way through the knot of men standing silently outside her tent.

"Eliza! Hold up, Lizzie!" George caught her around the waist, holding her back when she would have thrown herself upon her husband's recumbent form. "Let Martha do what she can."

Sobbing, Eliza collapsed onto George Sampson's chest, stifling her sobs.

"Tell me George. Please tell me he'll be all right," she pleaded, sobbing when her friend shook his head.

"I can't do that, Lizzie. It wouldn't be true. Jason was hurt bad when the roof of the shaft caved in. He's alive, still, but only just."

"Will ...Will he die, George?" Eliza whispered. "Is Jason going to die?"

No-one answered, but the silence, and the men's eyes looking everywhere but at her, told Eliza the truth. Her husband was dying.

"Let me go to him, George. Please."

Fighting for composure, Eliza crept into the tent to kneel beside Martha Stubbs, midwife and the nearest thing to a doctor to be found in this Godforsaken place. She peered intently into her husband's ashen face. His bright eyes closed.

"Here you are, dearie," Martha murmured. "You hold his hand and talk to him nicely. No tears, mind. There'll be time enough later for tears."

"J...J...Jason?" Eliza whispered, her mind going blank. Did it matter what she said, since he lay unresponsive to the goings-on around him? Could he hear her, even? "I love you Jason. So very, very much. Do you remember the day we met? That was the luckiest day of my life. "

She didn't know how long she knelt by Jason's side, reminding him, and herself, what they meant to each other, but finally, mouth dry from talking, Eliza ran out of words. A tiny sob escaped her lips, but she gulped back those which sought to follow in a flood.

"You're doing fine, lass," Martha murmured. "He hears you. Your voice is keeping him calm." She put a pannikin of tea someone passed in from outside the tent into Eliza's hands. "Wet your throat, now, then keep up the good work."

The baby. He doesn't know yet. I'll tell him about our baby.

So Eliza told him the secret she'd been saving for their evening alone together, using every ounce of acting ability she possessed to sound happy and excited.

From the baby she went on to tell Jason about the home they would have one day soon, but after a bit she lapsed into a silence where the only sound was her husband's harsh, rattling breath.

Casting around in her mind for a new topic, Eliza was startled when the hand she held squeezed hers. Weak as it was, it was the first response Jason had made to her presence. Slowly, his eyes opened, his dull, brown gaze fixed on her face.

"Lizzie. Sweet Lizzie." Jason's voice, thready and weak, was barely audible. Eliza leaned closer, smiling through her tears. They were all wrong. Jason was waking up. He was going to be all right.

"Find someone ... good, Lizzie. Take care ... baby ... and you. Be ... brave. Do what ... ye ... must."

On the last word, Jason seemed to slump in on himself.

Exhausted, Eliza tried to tell herself. *He's exhausted from talking.*

But it was a lie.

Martha, who'd had her fingers on his other wrist, shook her head and laid the hand she held across Jason's chest. With a tender gesture, she closed the eyes which had remained locked on Eliza's face past his last breath.

Rising stiffly to her feet, Martha trod heavily out of the tent, pulling the flap down behind her.

"Move back, you lot," she ordered those standing vigil outside. "Give the lass some time alone to say goodbye to her man."

HOME IS THE HEART

10

New Norcia, March, 1889.

Numb with shock and grief, it was only the need to be strong for his children which kept Sean functioning normally. On the outside, at least. On the inside it was another story altogether. Ann's perfume pervaded the air in the bedroom they had shared, making it impossible for him to be in it with her gone. Throughout their home everything his eye fell upon reminded him of Ann, the pain of her loss unbearable.

In desperation, he removed himself to a previously unused guest room and, after the first aimless days, spent every waking moment he could out in the paddocks, working himself into exhaustion in an attempt to keep his memories at bay. Without his beloved Ann, Sean's life became a sad, dull progression of empty days and sleepless nights.

The day after Fr Martinez, the parish priest for New Norcia, conducted Ann's funeral, a grief-stricken Humphrey Jackson carried his wife back to their own home.

Sedated following the accident, it was deemed necessary to administer regular doses of laudanum to control her excessive outpourings of grief. Everyone hoped she would improve once removed from the scene of the tragedy.

Sean couldn't wait to see the back of them.

If Augusta had only left her useless bloody dog behind, my Ann would still be with us, he raged silently, seeking to apportion blame for what had been a tragic accident.

Joan Smith, wife of his headman, Billy Smith, became a solid pillar of support to Sean, caring for the girls when he couldn't be with them. She continued to keep the house according to her mistress's instructions, and even supervised Mary and Judith in the simple lessons he set them in an attempt to keep them to their regular routine. Without her practical common sense, Sean would have been lost indeed.

"You'll need to get someone in to take charge of the girls," Humphrey had told him, shaking his hand in farewell. Meaning a white woman, of course, but although Sean had agreed, Joan coped so well he felt no urgency to comply.

He didn't want some strange woman taking up residence in Ann's house, telling him how to bring up his children. He wanted his Ann back.

Then, when friends and neighbours began prodding him to employ a housekeeper, or even a governess, he reluctantly placed advertisements in the newspapers, there being no-one suitable in their immediate area.

He even arranged interviews with the most promising applicants.

However, the only women willing to accept a position out in the bush, in the home of a single man, were not women Sean could accept as mentors to his girls. Weeks became months and still the situation remained unresolved.

Until, near the end of February, Augusta and Humphrey Jackson arrived unannounced to find Mary and Judith playing with Joan Smith's two boys, Peter and Paul. Barefoot, their faces and clothes liberally smudged with dirt, hair in disarray, they were having they time of their lives learning to track the wild creatures living in the bush near their home.

Joan and Polly, up to their elbows in suds, were fully occupied with the weekly laundry, happy to let the children amuse themselves till they were finished.

Not so the Jacksons. Even Humphrey, normally the most even-tempered of men, was outraged to see his granddaughters cavorting around the bush in the company of native children.

"What is Sean O'Grady thinking of, neglecting my Ann's children like this!" Augusta stormed, knowing precisely where to lay the blame. "You, woman. Yes, you, Smith. Bath these children immediately and dress them decently," she ordered, stomping through the house looking for non-existent signs of further slovenliness.

"Yes, Mrs Jackson," Joan replied, "but they was only playin' outside till Polly and me finished the washin', then we were gunna tidy them up for when their father comes in for his dinner."

"How dare you answer me back!" Joan cowered away from the walking stick in Augusta's raised hand.

"When you've done that, start packing their things. They'll be going home with us. Now get to it! We've no time to waste."

Hurrying to obey the irate being who'd invaded the homestead, Joan whispered to Polly to send the boys for the Boss as they called Sean.

"He won't be likin' this, he won't, Polly. Not one little bit." Shaking her head, Joan hustled the girls into the bath-house and filled the tin tub. Taking her time about it, she'd only just begun to fill a chest from the storeroom with the girls' possessions while the Jackson's waited in the sitting room with the refreshments Polly had rustled up, when Sean arrived.

"Humphrey! Augusta!" Sean rushed in, forgetting in his haste to remove his dusty work boots. "You should have told me you were coming. I'd have had Joan prepare your room."

"Humph! No need to put yourself out. I reckon it's a good thing we did come on the spur of the moment. This way we got to see your disgraceful neglect of our granddaughters. They'll be coming back with us, just as soon as that black slattern packs their bags."

Sean, already guilty he hadn't given them the welcome Ann would have considered their due, felt winded, as if from a blow to the gut. The Smith boys had said only that the Jackson's had arrived. He'd had no forewarning of impending disaster.

Take my girls?

Over my dead body!

Tempted to simply throw them out of his house and send them on their way, a warning voice whispered in his mind to take a more cautious approach or he could end up the loser.

"Now, Augusta, There's no need for that. This is my girls' home. They'll be staying right here with me, where they belong. You're both welcome to visit at any time, though, as I've said before." He had, although he'd hoped distance would severely restrict such visits.

"They belong in a decent Christian home, not running wild with a mob of blacks. You had your chance, Sean O'Grady. Ann would turn over in her grave if she could see what they've been reduced to!"

"Sean, my boy," Humphrey stepped in to ward off the angry reply he saw coming. "Normally I'd have no hesitation in agreeing that children belong with their parents, that is, with you. Their father. But surely you must concede, Augusta has a point. You promised us you'd get a woman in to take care of the girls, but there's no sign of one. Did you even try?"

"Of course I did! I'm still trying, only it's not an easy thing to find a reputable woman willing to come this far out from Perth to work as a governess. In the meantime, Joan and Polly are doing an admirable job of caring for Mary and Judith."

"Admirable! You … You …" Augusta spluttered, rage momentarily overcoming her ability to form a cohesive sentence. But only momentarily.

"We're leaving immediately, Sean O'Grady, and we're taking our granddaughters with us."

"You can leave when you like, but Mary and Judith stay here. They're my children, and they'll be staying with me."

"Now, Sean, be reasonable." Humphrey once again attempted to pour oil on the troubled waters.

"They'll be better off with us. Just until you get your situation sorted out. Then they can return."

For the next hour, the argument raged back and forth, neither side giving an inch. In the end, the Jacksons, defeated, piled back into their carriage and drove off in a huff. Without the girls who stood either side of their father on the verandah, waving them off.

"Don't think you've heard the last of this, Sean O'Grady," Augusta yelled, getting in the last word, "because you haven't."

11

The road west from Southern Cross, March, 1889.

On the sixth of March, two days after burying her husband, Eliza bought a seat on a wagon heading west in the morning. Not the carriage Jason had promised her, but, with a baby on the way, conserving her funds was more important than comfort.

Eliza had her reservations about the driver of her wagon, but took reassurance from knowing she wasn't the only female passenger. Besides, she had learned not to judge by appearances. Some of the wildest, scruffiest men on the goldfields had turned out, on closer acquaintance, to be perfect gentlemen.

It was to be hoped Tom Griggan proved likewise, as she wasn't prepared to waste her meagre resources on exorbitantly priced accommodation in Southern Cross till something, make that someone, better presented himself.

George had been generous in buying out her share of the mine, but her bankbook was still too lean. She'd need to find work, soon, and hoped the references from Sam Jones would help.

With her friends, George Sampson and Sam Jones assisting her, Eliza had sold everything she couldn't carry in Jason's large canvas backpack. It cost quite a pang to part with Jason's tools, meant to be used in building their new life, but they were simply too heavy for her to manage, and with the baby coming, their monetary value trumped their sentimental value.

"Do what you must," Jason had said, so she did.

*****

Bone-weary, her head aching, Eliza heaved a sigh of relief on climbing down from her perch in the back of the wagon on arrival at their first night's camping spot. Tom Griggan had offered her the more comfortable seat up front beside him, but she had been disinclined to accept since his overly-familiar manner made her uncomfortable in an altogether different way. Being jolted along like a sack of potatoes, breathing in the dust churning up from the wheels, still seemed preferable to his dubious company.

Neither had she found anyone else among her travelling companions whom she deemed congenial. They were a coarse, rowdy lot, women as well as men.

Eliza sighed again.

Perth seemed a very long, lonely ride ahead.

Food was provided, only they had to cook it themselves.

While they men scavenged for firewood and conferred with the others sharing the campground while they filled the water bottles, Eliza took her place with the other women on kitchen duty. When it came time to lay out the bedroll she'd strapped to her pack, she chose a spot as close as she could to some respectable families from the east-bound group. A safe distance away from Tom Griggan who seemed unable to take his eyes off her.

I'll be finding other transport once we reach Northam, Eliza decided, even if it meant forfeiting the remainder of her fare. Sometimes other considerations outweighed financial benefits. *Or maybe I'll be really lucky and find work there instead of going all the way to Perth.*

She added an extra plea to Jason to watch over her to the silent prayers she sent Heavenward, in the direction of the Southern Cross constellation sparkling in the black velvet sky above them. Ever since George Sampson had pointed it out from the myriad stars comprising the Milky Way, she'd found herself seeking it out until now it had the feel of an old, familiar friend.

The second day was a repeat of the first, except that when they reached the campground the best places were already taken.

"I know a good spot a couple of miles further on, mates," Tom Griggan informed them. "Just get those water bottles filled, an' we'll keep on."

It sounded reasonable, but away from the company of others, Eliza's companions lost far too many of their inhibitions for her comfort.

After dinner, bottles of cheap grog appeared, and were passed from mouth to mouth around the group, the women included. Only Eliza, jeered at for being stuck-up, declined. Bawdy stories became progressively more risqué in proportion to the lowering of the levels in the bottles until Eliza, red-faced with embarrassment, felt her cheeks would never return to their normal pale tones.

In desperation, she took herself off to bed. Which produced another dilemma. She couldn't remain near the warmth of the campfire, but nowhere else felt safe either.

Thank the Lord we arrive in Northam tomorrow.

Debating where to lay out her bedroll, Eliza gave a sharp scream when Tom Griggan emerged at her side out of the darkness.

"Two minds with the same thought," he slurred. "Time to stop playin' hard ta get, woman. Ya need ta be a bit more sociable, like. Gi'mee a kiss, then."

Ducking away from his attempted grab, Eliza tripped on the rough ground. On her like a shot, Tom Griggan began pawing at her clothes, inflicting slobbering kisses on her cheeks when she strove to avert her lips from his assault. Scrabbling to escape, her hand landed on a knobbly, fist-sized rock, her fingers closing on it automatically.

Without stopping to think, Eliza swung the rock in a wide arc, desperately smashing it against Griggan's head with all her strength. Then, when his grip loosened, she did it again.

His yelp of pain cut off abruptly by her second blow, Griggan slumped upon her, pinning her beneath him.

Fighting free of him, Eliza struggled to her feet. Her groggy attacker began showing signs of recovery, so Eliza used the rock in her hand again. This time Tom Griggan lay prostrate at her feet.

Wasting no time, Eliza snatched up her bag, determined to put as much distance as she could between herself and Griggan. *And those mates of his,* she added, hearing a raucous voice raised in song over by the fire. At the last moment she remembered the water bottles.

Without Tom Griggan's wagon she'd be afoot and would need every drop she could carry. Drinking her fill first, she ditched her books, though not without a pang, replacing them in her pack with extra water bottles. Then, carrying two more in her hands, she turned to go.

To be confronted by Tom Griggan stirring to life. Roaring out his rage, shaking his aching head down which Eliza saw a trickle of blood, he was struggling to push himself upright. A bull of a man, Eliza was terrified of what he'd do to her if he caught her. Backing away, she began praying frantically. Oh, how much she needed Jason at this very minute. With Jason, alive and well, at her side, she'd never needed to fear the likes of Tom Griggan.

"Kick 'im Lizzie! Kick 'im while he's down!"

"Jason!"

Eliza stood stock-still, awestruck to hear her husband's beloved voice in her head. Then she took in his words. Circling around to come behind the beast on the ground, she did as he bid her, feeling her feet were directed by other than herself.

That was when Eliza discovered the masculine, steel-toed work boots she wore were good for more than protecting her feet from the rough ground. Three solid kicks to Griggan's head put him down again. The two extra to his ribs for good measure brought a chuckle to the guardian voice in her mind along with a parting instruction she didn't need to have repeated.

"Now git, Lizzie. Foller the stars."

*****

"Follow the stars is all very well," Eliza grumbled to herself, leaning back against a sheltering salmon gum tree for a rest, "only what do I do when the stars set?"

Which would happen very soon now.

She thought she knew how to use the Southern Cross as a compass, but in the dark, stumbling over uneven ground and around trees and gullies, she was afraid she may have strayed off course. *The moon,* she realised. *The moon goes from east to west across the sky. I'll follow it when my stars disappear.*

Tired as she was, a longer rest was so tempting, but not knowing how far she'd come, Eliza forced herself to her feet again. Her escape would all be for nothing if Griggan and his mates tracked her down. She shuddered. Griggan would probably kill her. That thought gave her pause. Had she killed him? Was she now a murderer?

But it was self-defence, she comforted herself, *and surely I'm not strong enough to kill a big, strong man like him anyway.*

There was nothing she could do, and no way was she going back to see. Always supposing she could find her way back. Eliza had an uncomfortable feeling she was well and truly lost.

Taking another sip of water, she struggled doggedly on. And on. Falling into a pattern of walking and resting, the hours ran into each other. The light of what she'd learned to call the piccaninny dawn caught Eliza by surprise.

Lowering her pack to the ground, she put her hands to the small of her back, easing the dull ache. Her back wasn't all that ached. Her legs trembled, and her feet burned. This was harder than the walking she'd done months back on the way to the goldfields, but she'd found her rhythm, and she was sure there'd be a lot more walking to come before she reached safety.

Another rest. Another drink, and she pushed wearily to her feet once again. It would get hot very quickly when the sun rose, so she'd go as long as she could then find somewhere to hide and sleep during the day. There'd been no sound of pursuit all night, but the main road to Northam was barred to her. That was where Griggan would be. However, Eliza was aware Northam lay in a band of farming country stretching to the north and south of the town. If she steered in a north-westerly direction, sooner or later she'd come across signs of habitation, and she had the sun, the moon and the stars to guide her feet.

*****

It was the third morning since Eliza had fled, and, at the end of her strength, she was afraid she and her baby were going to become food for the wedge-tailed eagles and crows. The last of her water was gone, and she'd had no food at all since that last dinner by the campfire. Light-headed, she'd been praying and praying as she automatically set one foot in front of the other.

However, she'd heard no more friendly voices in her head telling her what to do.

Deciding not to give up while she still had breath in her body, Eliza hoisted her much lightened pack for the last time and plodded on, marvelling at how easily she had parted with many of the items she'd once thought indispensable. Now she carried only important documents and a change of clothes. Even the frames holding the photos of Jason and her parents had been discarded as too heavy.

It was really too hot for walking, but, light-headed from hunger and thirst, Eliza's feet moved without conscious direction until some instinct made her focus. She was on a narrow animal pad. A path made by hoofed creatures, not kangaroos.

Hooves meant domesticated animals.

Hope renewed, Eliza staggered on, following the direction the animals had gone. A short way along there were droppings, still moist. She had to be close. Raising her head, she shaded her eyes with her hand, studying the land around her. Not far away she made out the shape of a wagon, its shape distorted by the heat-haze.

There were people near it. And sheep.

For one heart-stopping moment she feared her enemies had found her, but was too desperate to care. Closer to, she realised the people she saw had dark skins. Then, she truly thought she was hallucinating when she detected two white men in long, black robes.

Dogs, scenting her on the breeze, began barking.

The people looked towards her, then began running.

With a whispered, "Thank you, God," Eliza collapsed, insensible, onto the ground.

HOME IS THE HEART

12

New Norcia, March 1889.

"I will, of course, make enquiries, Mrs Baker, although to my certain knowledge, there are no suitable employment opportunities in the immediate vicinity for a young woman in your circumstances." Father Bernardo Martinez, the parish priest of New Norcia, patted Eliza's hand.

Blindly, Eliza lifted her eyes, looking towards the monastery buildings from where she sat with the good Father outside the Abbey Church.

When monks from New Norcia, shepherding their flock of sheep from waterhole to waterhole, had rescued her from certain death, she'd mistakenly believed all her troubles were over. The kindness with which she was received by Abbot Salvado had filled her heart with hope. Promising she would be cared for, he had handed her over to Fr Martinez who had found her congenial lodgings with an elderly couple, Mr and Mrs Fraser, there being no guest house in the monastery itself.

Now, fully restored to health, she had confided her full story to the priest, asking his help in finding a position where not only herself, but her unborn child, also, would be welcome.

It had been a forlorn hope at best, that she might find something here in the warm, kind-hearted community which had grown up alongside the Mission founded by Spanish Benedictine monks. Eliza had been buoyed up by the sense of homecoming she had experienced on her arrival, and which persisted still.

I could be happy here, she thought again, as she had numerous times over the last two days. Unfortunately, her need to support herself would be taking her away. Her longing for a home of her own had never been so strong.

"Naturally," Fr Martinez continued, drawing Eliza out of her musings, "I will furnish you with letters of introduction should you decide to remove yourself from our care."

"Oh, Father. I don't want to leave. Not for one minute, but I'm afraid I'll have no choice. The money in my bank account," for which she gave thanks for Jason's forethought, "won't last for long if I don't have work. The Frasers, lovely, kind people though they are, can't be expected to keep me indefinitely."

"True, my dear, but you know, it might be better for you to marry again, even though it is still so soon since you lost your husband, rather than looking for work. There are many who would seek to take an unholy advantage of a pretty young widow such as yourself."

Her life on the goldfields, living cheek-by-jowl with her neighbours, separated only by canvas walls, had left Eliza with few illusions.

She had no difficulty whatsoever understanding the 'unholy advantages' the priest alluded to so delicately, and a shudder rippled through her body at the thought of being forced to make a living on the streets of Perth, at the mercy of men such as Tom Griggan. That was no life, either for herself or her baby. She'd rather have died in the bush.

"You may be right, Father," she replied, once the shock of his suggestion eased, allowing her to speak coherently again, "but chance would be a fine thing."

"Chance, or the Hand of God. You must have faith, child." Father Martinez smiled, and patted her hand again.

"It so happens, I know of a good man who has tragically lost his wife. He needs the help of a decent, respectable woman to raise his two daughters. He is looking for a governess, but for you to go and live in his house without the presence of another woman would be utterly scandalous. He may, however, consider marriage an acceptable alternative."

Eliza's jaw dropped. The priest's 'good man' might consider marriage to a stranger acceptable, but the very idea repelled her. She stared, wondering if this kindly priest was in his right mind.

Eyes twinkling merrily, he smiled back at her.

"You think me a little crazy, but I assure you, Mrs Baker, the marriage I am suggesting would solve both your problems very neatly. You would have a home for your child, and he would have a loving mother for his daughters. Do not, I beg you, dismiss the possibility out of hand. Pray on it, and leave the rest to God."

Her mind awhirl, Eliza watched Fr Martinez, children gathering about the skirts of his cassock, walking away from her down the village street.

Marriage!

As Fr Martinez said, it would, of course, solve her problem. But it was too soon! It felt like yesterday she had seen Jason lowered into his grave. A tear trickled down her cheek, and she wiped it away, her mind in turmoil. How could she do it? Having known no other man than Jason whom she had loved, how could she bear another man's possession of her body?

Maybe, she thought, timidly considering her alternatives. *Maybe if he was kind.*

And considerate.

Other women married men they did not love, and managed to be happy. And she would, after all, have her memories to comfort her. *And my baby,* she added, wrapping protective arms around her body.

Her mind in turmoil, Eliza entered the Abbey Church, her eyes immediately drawn to the portrait of Our Lady of Good Counsel. She had been told the story of how, faced with certain destruction, Abbot Salvado had held this very image of God's Holy Mother in front of the bushfire bearing down on New Norcia. The desperate prayers of the whole community had been answered by a sudden change in the wind direction; a miracle of salvation.

The Mother of Good Counsel, this portrait of Our Lady was titled, and good counsel was what Eliza needed so badly. If only her own mother lived to advise her.

She felt so terribly alone.

Lighting a candle, she knelt to pray. When she ran out of words, she simply knelt there, her heart and mind open to the peace and serenity, and the faint whiff of incense, in the church.

In her mind, she once again heard Jason's last words to her. He had told her to find someone to care for her and their baby. And he had told her to do what she must.

Fr Martinez offered me a solution.

Of course, the priest's 'good man' might not want me, Eliza reminded herself a moment later, but if he did, she'd be a fool not to consider accepting.

The candle was guttering, and the morning almost gone before Eliza stirred, rising stiffly from the pew to leave her sanctuary.

*****

"Just the one for you today, Mr O'Grady." The postmistress reached for the letter she had not long before slotted into its pigeonhole. "An important missive, I have no doubt."

She turned it over curiously, as if reluctant to part with the expensive embossed envelope.

"*Curtis, Curtis and Lambourne*," she read aloud the company name in the top corner. "They sound like lawyers to me. Good news, I hope, Mr O'Grady, although, in my experience, lawyers are more often the bearers of sad tidings."

Sean's blood ran cold. *Curtis, Curtis and Lambourne,* names very familiar to him, were indeed lawyers.

He had often had occasion to meet with them during his years as Humphrey Jackson's farm manager. Why the Devil was John Curtis writing to him? With Augusta's recent threats still ringing in his ears, he was all too afraid he could guess at the reason.

"I have no idea," he muttered, reaching impatiently to claim his mail from the postmistress. The envelope finally in his possession, he made a hasty farewell and strode out of the Post Office, tearing it open and unfolding the several pages contained within it.

What he read halted him in his tracks. Face blanching, he swayed on his feet, trying to absorb the meaning of the words. It couldn't be! They couldn't do that! Could they?

He stared blindly into space, unaware of his surroundings until Jim Short, a neighbouring farmer, clapped a hand on his shoulder, startling him.

"You orright, Mate? Not bad news, is it?" he nodded to the pages Sean gripped tightly.

"No. No, just something a bit unexpected."

Realising Jim wasn't the only one beginning to take undue notice of him, Sean quickly stuffed the letter into the inside pocket of his jacket and made his apologies. He needed to find somewhere more private to study what was, not simply a letter, but a legal threat to remove his children from his custody.

An unfit parent, Augusta Jackson had labelled him. His blood boiled at the unfairness of her insult.

Without direction, his feet led him to the cemetery. To Ann.

Over the months following her death, Sean had fallen into the habit of taking his problems to Ann. Telling her of his troubles seemed, somehow, to diminish them. Make them more manageable. Although he doubted even Ann could help him today.

This problem was a direct result of his loss of her living presence in his life. And, more to the point, in their daughters' lives. And he was right.

Reading the threatening communication aloud to Ann had done nothing to help. It merely confirmed the helplessness of his position. He would have to do something, and fast, but what? His advertisements had yielded no suitable applicants for the position of governess to his daughters, so he couldn't see the point of advertising again, now speed was of the essence.

His case would be heard in Court the next time the District Magistrate made his regular rounds of the rural towns. All Sean could think to do was to go to Perth himself in the hope of finding a suitable woman.

"I won't give up, Annie. I promise. I'll do whatever it takes to save our girls."

The voice whispering in the back of his mind that he'd left it too late made him feel even more defeated.

Sighing heavily, he put the letter away again and pushed himself to his feet, only then noticing Fr Martinez, the parish priest, standing at a polite distance, waiting for him.

*****

"Ah. Sean. I had been hoping to have a word with you soon. How goes your quest to find a governess for your little girls?"

"Badly, Father. The chance you might have heard of someone was my last hope. I don't suppose …?"

"Alas, no. My enquiries have not borne fruit."

Sean groaned in despair, clutching his head with both hands.

"What is it? My son," Fr Martinez placed a gentle hand on Sean's shoulder. "Has something else happened to plague you? Tell me what it is, for your people have a saying, do they not, that a problem shared is a problem halved?"

"Unfortunately, Father, since you are unable to assist me in the matter of finding a governess, I doubt there is much you can do to help, other than pray for me."

"Always, my son. But you should not discount the power of God to offer an unexpected solution."

His heart heavy, Sean shared the news of the latest calamity to befall him.

"… so you see, Father, unless a miracle happens, I fear that with the sanction of the Court, the Jacksons will steal my children from me. All because I have only black servants."

"It is indeed a pity so few settlers are not more tolerant of the native Australian peoples," Fr Martinez agreed, silently asking his Lord's guidance in what he was about to suggest. "While you and I both know your children are in no danger in Joan Smith's capable hands, I fear we shall have to comply with social expectations if you are not to lose your little Mary and Judy."

The two men sat side by side on the log, one sunk in the depths of despair, the other marshalling his words, determined to do well by his friend.

"Perhaps you should be looking for a wife, Sean, instead of a governess? A wife would solve your problem permanently."

"I have no time to go courting, Father. Indeed, I have no heart to do so either, and even if I did, who is there for me? I've been thinking of making a trip to Perth to throw myself on the mercy of friends, but time is running out."

Sean straightened, adjusting his hat on his head. He ought not to be wasting time with the priest with so much to do.

"Walk with me," Fr Martinez asked. "Just as far as the church. Did you hear our news, Sean? About the miraculous rescue of a woman lost in the bush?"

Sean hadn't, and, truth to tell, at the moment he had little interest in local gossip, but he and the priest were going in the same direction, so he listened politely while his friend recounted the tale of Mrs Eliza Baker, the young widow who'd strayed from the road, becoming lost, to be found by the monks.

"You must meet her, Sean, my friend," Fr Martinez urged. "She is in great need of a good man to give a home to her and her unborn child. You could help each other. Of course, with a decent young woman such as Mrs Baker, you would have to offer marriage, but after all, your need is most urgent."

He said not another word, letting Sean absorb his suggestion, but he prayed silently as they walked along the road.

God had provided the ideal solution for both the young people, if only they could be brought to see it for themselves.

13

New Norcia, April, 1889.

Making the sign of the Cross, Eliza took a steadying breath. This was it. No going back now.

Patting her hand when she rested it on his arm, portly, silver-haired Mr Fraser, who had claimed the right to stand in place of a father and give her away, whispered in her ear.

"You're doing the right thing, lass. For yourself, and Sean O'Grady's two little girls as well. Just you remember that when you feel in doubt."

When I feel in doubt! I've felt little else since Fr Martinez suggested to us that we should marry for the sake of the children. Hysterical laughter bubbled in Eliza's chest, but she refused to give way to it.

The time for turning back long gone, Eliza nodded, and steeled herself to take a new husband in her beloved Jason's place.

She had made Sean O'Grady a promise, and she'd see it through. For the children. Dear Lord, but she was shortly going to be a mother to *three* children when she'd barely got used to the idea of one. God had granted her wish for a home and a family, even if not in quite the manner she'd been imagining. Now it was up to her to build on His gift.

Eliza raised her eyes, and began the slow march down the aisle on Mr Fraser's arm. Wilfred Lane, an elderly chap who played his violin at local dances, played a slightly off-key *Ave Maria* for her. And there Sean O'Grady, tall and broad, solid and dependable as English oak, waited at the altar. For her. She devoutly hoped he was the 'good man' Fr Martinez had claimed him to be.

*****

They had met only the once, she and Sean O'Grady, on the day kindly Fr Martinez introduced them to each other. Disappearing on business of his own, he'd left them to come to an agreement on their own. Or not. For what felt like the longest time, they'd stood silently outside the Abbey Church, assessing each other with surreptitious sidelong glances.

Sean turned his hat in his hands, wondering what to say. He understood his friend's reasoning, was even desperate enough to give it a try, but how did a man propose marriage to a woman he'd never laid eyes on before?

"Father says he's talked to you about my situation," Sean had begun, speaking jerkily, embarrassed to be having such an intimate conversation with a woman who was a complete stranger. At least she was giving him a hearing, not storming off as he'd been afraid she might.

"What he didn't know then was that it has worsened. My parents-in-law have applied for custody of my girls, and as matters stand, they'll likely win. Fr Martinez is of the opinion marriage will ensure the children remain with me."

"Oh, dear. Mr O'Grady, that's simply dreadful. You must be so worried."

"Goes without saying." Sean kicked at the dirt, his voice unnaturally gruff. "The thing is, Mrs Baker, if we're to go along with this idea of marriage, it will have to happen almost immediately, or it will be too late to serve my purpose."

Eliza gasped. She'd been thinking of several weeks, maybe even a month or two, in the future, giving them time to get to know each other first. Accustom themselves to the idea.

Do what you must, Lizzie.

Jason's voice echoed in her mind. Encouraged, though shaking in her boots, she lifted her head, meeting Sean O'Grady eye to eye, striving to see beyond his face to the character within. Nothing she saw set alarm bells ringing, so, swallowing her fears, she proceeded with the negotiations.

"Did he tell you about my baby?" she asked, determined to be totally honest. "I wouldn't be considering a second marriage so soon after my husband's death except for the baby, you know. I'm not afraid to work hard to support myself."

"He did. I would naturally adopt your child and raise it as my own."

Anything less and I wouldn't be having this discussion, Eliza thought, hoping this man was as good as his word.

They had talked for a while longer, sharing information about their lives, until Fr Martinez reappeared, walking in their direction. Taking a deep breath, Sean turned to Eliza, taking her hands in his.

"So, Mrs Baker. How about it," Sean asked. "Will you do me the honour of marrying me and caring for my daughters?"

Unexpectedly, he found himself holding his breath while awaiting her answer. Eliza Baker was a good-looking woman. Certainly too young and pretty to have to fend for herself. Her baby wasn't showing itself yet, her waist still very trim, but it wasn't her blonde hair pulled back into a prim bun, or her pale blue, very direct eyes which had his pulse speeding the blood through his veins, Sean assured himself.

Thinking of bedding Eliza Baker, which he couldn't help doing, with all this talk of marriage, smacked of disloyalty to his Ann. Appealing to his senses though Eliza Baker was, he would never have looked twice at her except that she represented the means of winning out over Augusta and Humphrey Jackson. Of keeping his girls safely in their own home, where they belonged. The only means available to him.

Firming his lips, he waited impatiently for her answer.

He would do whatever it took.

Heart racing, refusing to be hurried, Eliza stared down at their joined hands, noting the scars and callouses on his, the products of working his land with his own hands. Honest labour, to be respected. Meticulously clean nails pleased her. He smelt clean, too, and she liked cleanliness in a man. Slovenliness would have turned her off immediately.

Sean O'Grady's obvious discomfort with the situation was also oddly reassuring. It would have been so unfair if she had been the only one nervous and uncertain of taking this step. Raising her eyes to meet his, she tried to smile, afraid it was a rather poor attempt.

"Yes, Mr O'Grady. I will be honoured to marry you."

With that black hair and blue eyes, he's really quite handsome, in a rugged sort of way.

Eliza felt her cheeks warming, and cast her eyes down once more. She shouldn't be noticing such things about him. About any man, while Jason still filled her heart, but she couldn't help wondering what those large, capable hands would feel like upon the private parts of her body. Would she enjoy the intimacies of the marriage bed with him as she had with Jason?

However, speculation did nothing beyond making her even more nervous. She had given her answer, and she would not renege. The marriage would by no means be one-sided, either. For purely practical reasons, Sean O'Grady needed her every bit as much as she needed him.

A thought reassuring to Eliza's pride.

*****

The arrangements for the wedding had been made that same morning, and two days later, ladies from all over the district had gathered in Mrs Fraser's parlour. Pauline Maguire, who had been Ann O'Grady's best friend, appointed herself spokeswoman.

"Mrs Baker. Eliza. We can call you Eliza, can't we?" she had asked, rattling on when Eliza murmured her consent.

117

"We all know the dreadful straits Sean is in, what with those in-laws of his putting all that pressure on him, and we're really grateful to you for coming to his rescue in the nick of time."

She's making me sound like some sort of heroine, Eliza thought, feeling anything but. However, she'd taken an immediate liking to the gregarious Pauline, so she kept her thoughts to herself.

"Normally the gifts at a bridal shower would be for your new home, only you'll have little need of such, since Sean's house is already properly equipped, so, knowing your circumstances, we've taken it on ourselves to help you with your trousseau."

Heat flooded Eliza's whole body. Shamed, she fixed welling eyes on her tightly clasped hands.

"Oh, dear. I'm sorry Eliza. That came out all wrong," Pauline gasped. "I only meant we all know how hard it is to put a trousseau together quickly out here in the bush. We want you to feel welcome, you know."

Other, equally friendly, voices murmured agreement.

"Please forgive me for thinking otherwise. I'm sure it's very kind of you. All of you." Still blushing, Eliza faced the group, dredging up a shaky smile.

Relieved, accompanying their offerings with friendly hugs and kisses, the ladies hastened to pass over their gifts. Perfume, scented soaps and other toiletries. Pretty handkerchiefs, and guest towels, a fine paisley shawl, nightdresses.

Particularly welcome was a delicate white blouse which Eliza knew would go well with her black skirt for the wedding day itself. Last of all was a straw bonnet, tastefully trimmed with artificial rosebuds. Not all the gifts were brand-new, but all were given with love. And all were items Eliza lacked.

"Oh, thank you all so much," She said, her voice trembling. "You're all so very kind. You know, I have the money to buy what I need, except that …"

"Except that our shop doesn't stock any but the most prosaic essential items and there's no time to send away for what you need," Mrs Fraser cut in. She'd already been shopping with Eliza and understood her predicament. Had, in fact, communicated it to her friends, resulting in these delightful gifts. "We all understand, dear. A bride deserves a few nice things to boost her confidence, even when it's not a love-match."

"Especially when it's not a love-match," chimed in Milly Partridge who'd made a marriage of convenience herself.

"Although," she added, blushing coyly, "that's not to say love won't grow, if you give it a chance."

*****

Will love grow between us?

Eliza wondered, placing her hand in Sean's as Mr Fraser stepped back and went to sit beside his wife on the front pew.

Shyly, she looked at her groom. Dressed in his best suit, Sean O'Grady looked every inch a gentleman. A very handsome gentleman, although not a patch on her Jason.

Confused, guilty, Eliza didn't know whom she betrayed most in her thoughts – Jason whom she had loved and lost, to whom she still gave her loyalty; or Sean, whom she might never love, but who now had the right to lay claim to that very same loyalty.

Looking again at their joined hands, images of the night to come when Sean would touch her with those hands, strayed into her mind. Feeling her cheeks heating, Eliza resolutely turned her attention to Fr Martinez.

Listening closely to the words, Eliza repeated her vows in a firm, clear voice, meaning every word now as she had the first time, when she had married Jason back in England.

An irrelevant thought to be popping into her mind at such a time, but Eliza realised she no longer thought of England as home.

Australia was home, now. She had a new country, a new marriage, new husband, and children she had yet to meet. On her way down the aisle, she had glimpsed two little girls nestled solemnly on the front pew at Mrs Fraser's side, wondering fleetingly if they would like her.

She did hope they wouldn't resent her too much for taking their mother's place.

"I now pronounce you man and wife. You may kiss your bride."

Eliza snapped back to attention, her pulse thudding as Sean O'Grady put a finger under her chin, lightly lifting her lips to meet his in the bridal kiss.

Their very first kiss.

The merest touch of Sean O'Grady's lips to hers, it was over almost before it began, leaving her strangely disappointed yet relieved, all at the same time.

In the vestry, Brian and Pauline Maguire witnessed their signatures, then Mrs Fraser kissed Eliza on the cheek.

"Here you are, my dear. I've brought Mary and Judith to congratulate their father and meet their new mother. What do you say, girls?"

Quelling a moment of panic, Eliza smiled a welcome, watching their father crouch down in front of the girls, wrapping his arms around the two of them and kissing each on the cheek.

"Hello Mama."

Eyes on the floor, the younger of the two muttered an almost inaudible greeting when prompted again by her father. Not so the elder.

"You're not my Mama!" she declared mutinously. "I don't want a new mother! I want my *own* mother!" Bursting into noisy sobs, she flung herself back into her father's arms, her sister soon sobbing in sympathy.

"Well, that's a fine thing to say, and no mistake." Mrs Fraser, hands on ample hips, prepared to defend her protégé while Pauline knelt beside Sean helping in his attempt to stem the floods of tears.

Shunted unceremoniously to one side, Eliza cast a panicked glance towards Fr Martinez as if to say, "You got me into this. What do I do now?"

Never one to back down from a challenge or to admit defeat, the priest took charge, ushering the witnesses back through the door into the church.

"I believe it will be best to leave our new family to sort themselves out without our assistance," he said, winking merrily at Eliza. "Time to show what you're made of, Mrs O'Grady," he whispered, passing close to her at the tail of his little procession.

Time to show what I'm made of!

And what is that, Eliza wondered, knowing this was a make or break moment in her future relationship with her step-daughters

She should begin as she meant to go on. Kind. Firm. With no mollycoddling.

Interrupting Sean's hushing murmurs, she pulled out two of her new embroidered handkerchiefs.

"Here we go. One for you, Judith, dear, and the other for Miss Mary, she said briskly, in a gentle, no-nonsense voice.

"You don't want the other children to laugh at you, so dry those pretty eyes and make your Papa and your real Mama proud of you. She's still watching over you, you know. She always will be. And, Mary, it's all right to miss your mother. I still miss mine, and she died a long, long time ago. It's up to you to be good for Papa, now. Perhaps you might find it easier to call me 'Mam'," she said, inspired by a memory of the Glossop children.

"It's a different name for a mother and that's what I am, a different kind of mother for you."

Eliza gave the children a moment to think over her offer.

"It's my place to help Papa take care of you now," she continued. "We'll have lots of time to get to know each other properly when we're at home."

Away from all these interested onlookers.

"Mam's right," Sean encouraged, using the suggested title quite naturally. "Remember how I explained to you why we need Eliza to take care of us?"

The girls nodded.

"So we don't have to live with Grandmama," Mary added. "I don't like Grandmama. She yells at us, and she hit me on my face when I broke the cup."

"Yes, well. We needn't go into that at the moment," Sean muttered, glad to see by her shocked gasp that Eliza found Augusta's actions as reprehensible as he did. "If we're all ready, let's show everyone how the O'Gradys are a family who stick together."

Hoisting a now smiling Judy to his shoulder, Sean took Eliza on his other arm. When she held out her free hand to Mary, Eliza was gratified to have the child clasp it tightly.

HOME IS THE HEART

14

"You looked very pretty today, Eliza."

"Thank you, Mr O'Grady." Eliza blushed. She had done her best, combining the little she already had with the gifts from the ladies, but knew she hadn't been the most fashionable or well turned out of brides.

"Oh, I think we can dispense with formality, don't you? I intend to call you by your given name, Eliza, and would appreciate your using my name."

Eliza blushed again. She already thought of her new husband as Sean, so that should not be difficult.

"Very well. Sean. I just want you to know, Mr … Sean, I will be the best wife to you that I can, and the best mother I can to Mary and Judith, also."

They were alone in the sulky, Pauline and Brian Maguire having taken the children home with them for the night.

"We arranged it yesterday, with Sean," Pauline laughingly informed Eliza.

"I thought the least we could do is give you a wedding night to yourselves. You deserved that much at least."

Little Judy had kissed her back when she farewelled them, but, although tolerating her kiss, Mary, holding herself aloof, had not returned it. Her heart sinking, Eliza hoped it was not a portent of their future relationship.

"You handled the children well. Ann would approve of your sensible approach to them. There's been far too much gushing and weeping over them and their motherless state, making them the constant centre of attention."

"I'm glad you think so. I merely did what seemed right. What my own mother would have done."

Her husband's approval was nice, only Eliza hoped very much she was not going to be compared to Sean's first wife at every turn. She already felt insecure enough.

"I can see Judith and Mary love you very much." Eliza, finding it difficult participating in their awkward conversation, wondered if he would be as loving a father to her baby as he was to his own children.

"It's wrong, what Mr and Mrs Jackson are trying to do," she added.

"Augusta has always been my enemy, but I did think better of Humphrey." Having Humphrey, whom he'd always viewed as a friend, turn on him had wounded Sean deeply. "Unfortunately," he explained to Eliza, "he's never been able to stand up to his virago of a wife."

Then Sean recalled another piece of information to share.

"I have written to my lawyers regarding our marriage, in the hope that we will now see the end of the Jackson's application for custody."

Eliza nodded, then, neither being able to think of a new topic of conversation, a stilted silence reigned, the horse trotting steadily on towards *Wattle Bend*.

"There it is, Eliza. Home." Sean pointed to where the corrugated iron roof of the house rose above the tops of the low trees bordering the track. He coughed, clearing his throat. The words he'd been trying to get out since they'd left the party at the Fraser's house seemed to be stuck in his throat, but the time to utter them was fast running out.

"Before we arrive, Eliza, there's something I need to say." Slowing the horse to a sedate walk, Sean cleared his throat again, pretending he'd swallowed a mouthful of dust. "It's not so long since your husband, since Jason, died." Sean forced himself to say the name of the unknown man he was afraid his very attractive new wife would forever compare him to, to his detriment. "Although it's a longer time since Ann died, we are both grieving still."

Eliza nodded, wondering where Sean was going with this speech. She didn't need to wait long to find out.

"I've decided we should wait before making this a true marriage. I thought, after your baby is born, will be soon enough. We'll know each other better by then, and it won't feel so strange to share a bed." He tugged at the neck of his shirt which suddenly felt far too tight, carefully avoiding the startled gaze of his new wife. "I'll sleep in the guest room till then," he muttered.

Stunned, Eliza gaped at him. She had steeled herself to accept her wifely duty, and now, he didn't want her! She didn't know whether to feel relieved or insulted.

"As you wish," she murmured, trying not to feel either.

Then they were driving into the yard of the stone and timber farmhouse, with the Aboriginal families who worked at *Wattle Bend* running to greet them; laughing, and calling out their welcome to the Boss and his new Missus.

*****

"Oh!" Eliza squeaked, taken by surprise when, without warning, Sean scooped her up in his arms to carry her across the threshold. She had not given the slightest thought to such traditional observances. After the bombshell he'd dropped on her just five minutes earlier, she couldn't help wondering cynically if he really meant it, or if it was merely a show he put on for their audience.

"Mr Sean," Joan Smith, the woman Sean introduced as her housekeeper, interrupted Eliza's less than happy thoughts. "You show the new Missus round the house, now, while I make tea." Not waiting for an answer, she bustled off in the direction Eliza surmised the kitchen lay.

"Yes, well. Come along, Eliza. It's quite a simple house, really. There's not much to it."

Simple, Sean had called it, and it was.

However, with a sitting room, dining room, parlour and five bedrooms in addition to the lean-to kitchen Sean said he'd leave to Joan to show her, Eliza suspected it was bigger than many farmhouses.

It was certainly bigger than the Fraser's house where she'd been staying, and, compared to her tent on the diggings, it was a palace.

"You have a lovely home, Sean," she said, quite sincerely, when they arrived back in the sitting room where Joan had set out the tea things for them.

They were the first words she'd spoken since entering the house. Sean's obvious discomfort when he carried her bag into the master bedroom, informing her gruffly that it was hers, then backing out to wait in the corridor till she emerged a few seconds later, had dried up the comments she had intended making.

That had been the room, the bed, he had shared with Ann, she realised, and, still in love with her, he'd been unable to bear seeing another woman in his wife's place. This insight made her feel guilty for her earlier uncharitable thoughts.

It wasn't until much later she had time to consider the fuller implications of that discovery. After conducting her on a quick tour of the gardens and outbuildings, Sean had taken himself off, supposedly to inspect the work done by Bill and Tommy.

"Maybe you'd like to unpack, Eliza," he'd suggested. "I'll see you at dinner. If you need anything, talk to Joan."

Obediently, Eliza had returned to her room.

Opening the wardrobe and chest of drawers, to put away her clothes, she had been appalled to find them full of Ann's dresses, coats and more intimate garments. The dressing table still contained the other woman's toiletries and jewellery. Her brushes and combs.

The only spaces were those once filled with Sean's things, where a light film of dust indicated he'd removed himself from this room a considerable time ago.

Has no-one touched a single thing? she wondered, daunted by the task awaiting her. There was no way she would ever be able to use a single one of these items, but she had no idea what to do with them.

In the interim, she carefully transferred all of Ann's things into the tiny bedroom adjoining hers which had been lovingly prepared as a nursery for the baby Ann had been expecting at the time of her death. And shut the door, knowing the problem had only been deferred, not resolved. Perhaps Pauline could advise her.

It was only now Mrs Fraser's chatter about 'poor Mr O'Grady's double tragedy' came back to her. No wonder he resented being forced to take a new wife. He had lost so terribly much.

I at least, still have my baby to fill part of the gap Jason's death left in my heart, Eliza reflected, resting a protective hand where only the slightest of bulges hinted at the treasure cocooned within.

The room cleared of its previous occupant; it took Eliza next to no time to find places for her meagre possessions. About to go in search of Joan, she fingered the beautiful handmade quilt on the bed. If not Ann's own work, it had certainly been another familiar, intimate item of Sean O'Grady's marriage.

On the spur of the moment, Eliza bundled up the quilt and swapped it for the one in the main guest room, the one Sean had not laid claim to.

Now, if her husband ever decided to enter her room, he wouldn't be met with such a barrage of reminders of the wife he'd loved.

*****

Curled up alone under the covers that night, Eliza felt a tear trickle down her cheek, and stuffed a corner of the pillow into her mouth to muffle the sobs which followed. Had any bride ever felt so dismally lonely on her wedding night? It was impossible not to compare tonight with the joy of her first wedding night, when she had been a welcome, beloved bride. In some strange way, she missed Jason more at this moment than she had since leaving the diggings.

All the same, she found herself grateful to Sean for the reprieve he'd granted her.

But this is not the way to go on, she chided herself. *Crying achieves nothing. My life with Jason is the past. I must look to the future, and my new life as a farmer's wife.* She couldn't quite call herself Sean O'Grady's wife. Not yet.

Drying her eyes, she let her mind drift to the events of her evening. After Joan had cleared away the dinner dishes, she had tentatively asked Sean about the routines of life on an isolated farm.

"Living on a farm so far from town is new to me, Sean. I'm depending on you to guide me. For instance, how do I go about buying material to make new clothes for the girls? I noticed Mary's dress was rather tight on her. Her shoes, too."

Running his hand through his hair, Sean had appeared guilt-stricken.

"I'm so sorry. I'm afraid I've been neglectful. It's just … Ann used to take care of all that sort of thing. A lot of things we need we order from Perth, using store catalogues."

Once prompted, he'd given her a rapid run-down of her duties, delivering so much information all in one go she was afraid she'd forget the half of it. At the end, he'd waved a hand at the neat little desk in the corner of the room.

"That's where Ann kept her accounts and a calendar of when things were due and all those other things you've asked about," he said, then abruptly changed the subject.

"The boys saw a snake in the garden this morning," he said, warning her to be careful. "It may still be somewhere close."

A snake! Eliza had heard numerous stories of the dangerous creatures, but had only once seen one, and that after it had been killed. She didn't think she'd fancy meeting one unexpectedly.

Conversation becoming desultory, Eliza decided to bring the difficult evening to an end.

"It's been a long day, Sean. If you don't mind, I think I'll go to bed."

Immediately jumping to his feet up as if relieved to be left on his own, he ushered her out the door, giving her an impersonal peck on the cheek.

"I'm sorry Eliza," he murmured, leaving her wondering what he was sorry for.

She wondered still, although she was afraid she could guess. She was needed at *Wattle Bend*, but she didn't feel entirely wanted.

The future is up to me, isn't it? If I want to be happy here at Wattle Bend, I'll have to work at making my own happiness.

Beginning by counting her blessings, Eliza drifted off to sleep.

Sometime later, Sean turned out the lamp and headed for his room. Of their own accord, his feet slowed, bringing him to a halt outside Eliza's door. An image of her blonde prettiness and enticing figure rose in his mind, his hand reaching out to take hold of the doorknob. He'd been painfully aware of her feminine presence all evening, half-regretting the promise he'd made her to wait. She was his wife. He was entitled to claim her body. Entitled, certainly. Unfortunately, it would be a poor way to begin a marriage, breaking his own promise. He pulled his hand back and hurried past her door before he could change his mind.

Roused by the sound of footsteps outside her door, Eliza opened an eye to squint at the clock on her bedside table. Assuming it was Sean making his own way to bed, she closed her eyes again and settled back into a deeper sleep. Though something about the moment struck her as odd, sleep reclaimed her before she identified exactly what.

HOME IS THE HEART

15

A combination of birdsong and a rooster crowing close by woke Eliza. For a moment she lay, savouring the snug warmth of her blankets in the early morning chill. The first rays of the rising sun, shining into her eyes through a gap in the curtains, brought her fully awake. Stretching, she looked at the clock, wondering what the time was. And recalled doing the same thing during the night when Sean's footsteps had penetrated her slumber.

How strange. Had Sean's footsteps really halted outside her door, or had she dreamed it?

Shaking her head, she reached for her dressing gown. Tea, she decided, then she'd dress. She didn't know what time the day began on the farm, but suspected it would be early. On the diggings, the stamper starting up for the day had been a reliable alarm clock. She wondered if here that noisy rooster would prove itself an equally reliable tocsin.

Washed and dressed, Eliza had just poured a cup from the pot of tea she'd brewed when her new husband, who was not yet her true husband, appeared in the doorway.

"Good morning Sean." Her cheeks warming, she made sure her voice was bright and cheerful. Welcoming.

"Eliza. There was no need for you to get up so early."

Why does he sound so put out, she wondered. Wasn't part of her job being in the kitchen ready to see to his culinary needs? He may have decided he didn't want her in his bed, but surely he expected her to fill the role of his wife in other ways?

"I'm an early riser," she replied, carefully changing her annoyed pout into a tepid smile which failed to reach her downcast eyes. "Can I pour a cup for you?" She gestured towards the kitchen teapot wrapped in its well-worn cosy.

Sean nodded, mentally kicking himself for driving the cheerfulness from Eliza's expressive face. The girl was doing her best in a difficult situation. It was up to him to meet her halfway. More than halfway.

"Yes please." He forced a smile to his lips. "I was about to put the kettle on myself, and here you are. You've beaten me to it." Coming into the room, he gave her another of those gentle, impersonal, pecks on the cheek.

"I didn't mean to sound churlish. It's simply that I'm not used to anyone else being about at this time. I usually fix my own breakfast. Joan feeds the girls later."

He held her chair, politely seating her first, then, carrying his cup to the head of the table, he drew out his own chair and sat down.

"You don't feel queasy in the mornings?" He asked a moment later, sounding genuinely curious. "Ann always felt terribly ill in the early months," he explained.

"I do, a little, but I've found a cup of tea settles my stomach nicely. Since I'm up, what would you like for breakfast? There's just the two of us today, so I'll eat with you."

Eliza, deciding this would be a good ritual to establish, intended to ensure she shared the breakfast table with *this* husband every morning, as she had with Jason. It would give them a few private minutes alone to get to know each other a little better.

Later in the day, they went to collect Mary and Judith from their visit to the Maguire's homestead, but before then Eliza had had a very satisfactory chat with Joan Smith concerning the running of the household, and had even had time for a cursory glance through the desk containing the household books. Her desk now, and its contents her responsibility.

It wasn't many days before Eliza established herself as mistress of *Wattle Bend;* house, garden and children showing tangible benefits from her attention. Joan and Polly happily took their lead from her, singing and laughing as they went about their tasks.

With the homestead and children occupying her days, Eliza now had plenty to talk to Sean about when they sat together in the evenings, and when they ran out of conversation, read in a companionable silence.

During the second week, a letter arrived from George Sampson in reply to the one she wrote telling him of her new circumstances.

It was with relief she read of his approval, having been afraid he would feel her sudden marriage a betrayal of his friend.

Instead, he praised her common sense and wished her well, reminding her to stay in touch.

"George was such a good friend to us both," she told Sean, wiping away a stray tear. It wasn't the only tear she'd shed since her marriage, but usually she kept her feelings under control until she was alone in her room. She liked her new life, she really did, but Jason's death was still a raw wound in her heart.

Sharing George's letter led to Eliza telling Sean more about her life on the goldfields than she ever had before. He looked at her with a deeper respect that night, impressed with her resilience and adaptability. His new wife was young and pretty, but also a hard worker who carried her weight, not the grasping opportunist he'd been afraid she might be. He'd been luckier than he considered he deserved.

On closer acquaintance, Eliza, also, was favourably impressed with her new husband, in particular with the close interest he took in his daughters' activities. Her own father, although affectionate, had been rather distant. "Don't disturb Papa," had been an oft repeated admonition of her mother's.

Eliza preferred Sean's warmer brand of parenting, especially when the girls' eager efforts to please him meant they worked harder at the simple tasks and lessons she set them, and were generally more obedient.

Not that sweet little Judy posed any problem; she had become Eliza's faithful shadow, holding her hand when they walked, and chattering away like a little magpie.

Mary's continued aloofness saddened Eliza.

However, she hoped that in time the child would grow more accepting of her presence.

It's early days yet, she reminded herself.

One morning, taking the children into the garden to pick vegetables for dinner, Eliza came face to face with the only bush creature she truly feared.

"Snake! Snake!"

At Judith's terrified scream, Eliza, heart pounding, scooped the frightened child up in her arms. Not knowing what else to do, she watched the slender, dark reptile slither away across the open ground, headed for the bush beyond the garden.

"Where's the snake?" Joan, ears attuned for cries of alarm, came running from the house, grabbing a long-handled shovel from outside the back door as she passed.

"Over there!" Mary, standing behind Eliza, a fistful of her skirt clutched in her hand, pointed excitedly. "Quick, Joan! He's getting away!"

Rooted to the spot, Eliza watched, amazed at the other woman's fearlessness as she pursued the snake.

As soon as she was close enough, Joan brought the shovel down in a mighty blow which broke the reptile's back. A second blow decapitated it, leaving a yard-long body writhing harmlessly on the ground.

"He a bad bloke, that snake. You watch out for him, Missus," Joan warned, leaning nonchalantly on the shovel admiring her handiwork.

"Oh, Joan. Thank goodness you were here," Eliza gasped, setting Judith back on her feet. "It was lucky the shovel was handy."

"Not lucky, Missus. Shovel always right there." She held it up, showing Eliza its sharpened edges. "This my snake stick. I get him, but handle too long for him to get me. Good, huh?"

"Very good." Smiling weakly, Eliza held a hand to her wildly beating heart. She offered a silent prayer of thanks for Joan's stalwart presence.

That incident made up Eliza's mind regarding a problem she'd been worrying over.

Part of the reason Sean had married her was to prevent his daughters being brought up running wild with the native children, but she didn't feel right stopping them from playing together. Peter and Paul Smith were delightful children, always happy and cheerful. Neither did she want to offend Joan, who was generous with her friendship.

She'd been meaning to discuss the issue with Sean, but made up her mind on the spot to handle it herself.

"You know, Joan," she said later, slicing beans while the other woman peeled potatoes, "Your boys should be learning their numbers and how to read and write. I'd like them to join in with the girls' lessons in the mornings, if you approve, then they can teach me, and the girls, about the bush in the afternoons."

"Good idea, Missus," Joan agreed. "Boys get better jobs if they read and write and learn numbers."

This new regime worked well.

Several days later, when Eliza noticed Joan sending the boys out to the paddocks with lunch for Sean and his men, as usual, she included herself and the girls on the expeditions, turning them into picnics.

The first time, Sean had stared at her, surprised she'd come so far from the house. When he saw how much the children enjoyed sharing their lunch with him, he willingly joined in, seeming to have as much fun as they did.

"That was a good idea of yours today, Eliza," he said that evening. "It's nice spending time with my girls. Particularly when I don't have to neglect my work to do so."

"I'm glad it's all right with you, Sean. The boys showed us how to track a goanna on the way home. We're learning all about the bush from them. There are so many birds and animals and plants which are new to me. I'm going to take a sketchbook with me in future, to make drawings."

A few days later, when Sean asked Mary what she had learned that day, his daughter surprised him, producing a story the children had made together in class about the tracks they had seen in the bush, and the creatures which made them.

"We made up the words," Mary explained, "and Mam helped with the pictures."

"I coloured the kangaroo," Judith added, pointing. "Can I read it to you, Papa?"

That evening when Sean said goodnight to Eliza, he accompanied his usual peck on the cheek with a warm hug.

"You're doing so well with the girls, Lizzie," he murmured. "I'm glad I married you."

With pleased surprise Eliza realised, *I'm glad too*.

Wattle Bend already felt like home to her, and the children had become her family. Sean, too, even if he did not yet feel like a proper husband. His adoption of her old nickname felt good, too.

It felt like belonging.

She hummed one of her favourite songs that night as she prepared for bed.

*****

A few days later the men arrived back at the homestead early to find Eliza, Polly, Joan and the children playing cricket together in the backyard.

"The ploughing's finished, so I've declared the rest of the day a holiday," Sean announced. "Can we join your game?"

The four children shouted with joy to have their fathers play, and later, game over, Sean had hoisted Judy onto his shoulder and slung an arm around Eliza.

"Come on girls, time for tea. I'm parched."

Half turning to reach a hand to Mary, Eliza was shocked by the quickly disguised fury contorting the girl's face.

"Hurry up Mary, love, or the lemonade will be all gone," Sean called.

When Mary, laughing and shouting victoriously, ran past them to be first at the table on the verandah, Eliza told herself she must have been mistaken. Until the child glanced at her from behind Sean's back, the laughter momentarily erased from her face and replaced with a look of patent dislike.

The next day Polly took the boys with her to visit their grandparents on her day off. Mary, Judith and Eliza, alone on the now customary picnic lunch, detoured to the creek to play on the way home.

"One moment, Judy," Eliza said, noticing a trailing bootlace. "Let me tie that up for you or you'll trip on it." The lace tied, she hugged Judy, kissing her on the cheek. "There you go, love. All safe again."

"Thank you, Mama," Judith said, kissing her back before running off to play.

"Don't you call her that!" Mary shouted at her little sister, hitting her on the arm and making her cry.

"She's not our Mama. Our Mama is dead!"

By now, both children were crying loudly. When Eliza rushed to comfort them, Mary pushed past, shoving her rudely aside and running off. Feeling it would be wise to give Mary some time to herself, Eliza confined her attentions to Judith, assuring her she had done nothing wrong.

Ready to go home some time later, Eliza looked for Mary, only then realising she had not yet returned.

"Mary! Mary, it's time to go home!"

When there was no answer, she took Judy by the hand and walked in the direction she'd seen Mary run off, calling as they walked, Judy joining in. Silence answered them.

"Do you think she went home on her own?" Eliza asked Judith, trying not to let her growing fear upset the little girl. "Let's go and see, shall we?"

But there was no sign of Mary at the homestead. Joan hadn't seen her.

"I been digging weeds in the garden, Missus. I'd a seen if she came past."

"Then she's still out there. You mind Judith, please Joan, and I'll go back to find her."

In spite of searching and calling up and down the creek, there was no sign of the missing child. Dread of poisonous snakes and deep waterholes haunting her, Eliza searched desperately on, finally deciding to see if Mary had gone back to where her father was working.

"I've lost, her, Sean," Eliza concluded on a sob. "I've looked everywhere but I can't find her."

"Hush, Eliza. We'll find her. She's more at home in the bush than you are. She won't have come to any harm." But Eliza could see he didn't mean it. Sean was as worried as she was.

"Bill." Calling over his headman, Sean explained the problem. "We need you to track her down for us, Bill. Quick as you can."

"Sure thing, Boss. We find Little Missy quick smart."

It was a little slower than 'quick smart', however Bill succeeded in tracking Mary's path to where he found her curled up in the hollow trunk of an old fire-ravaged gumtree where she'd deliberately hidden from Eliza.

"That was very naughty of you, Mary. Very naughty."

Sean looked unaccustomedly grim. "You owe everyone an apology."

Hands on hips, he waited, outstaring his recalcitrant daughter. Finally, Mary dropped her eyes, scraping the toe of her boot in the dirt.

"I'm sorry," she muttered.

She didn't sound very sorry to Eliza, or to Sean either. He continued staring at her a while longer, then sighed and turned to Eliza and Bill who stood silently beside him.

"Bill, thanks for your help. You go back to the paddock and help Tommy finish up."

"Orright, Boss." Bill turned and loped off.

"Eliza." Sean turned to his wife. "Do you think you can find your own way home?"

She nodded.

Frowning, he turned back to his daughter.

"Mary and I need to have a little talk," he said, leading the child to a fallen log and sitting down. "We'll be along shortly."

Eliza, unsure how she felt at her summary dismissal, trudged off. It was over an hour later that father and daughter trod heavily across the yard to where Eliza and Judy sat reading on the verandah.

"You're a good girl, Judy. How about you help me collect the eggs? Mary has something to say to Mam."

Sean led Judith away, leaving Eliza and Mary staring uneasily at each other. Declining to give way to her anger, Eliza waited, hands folded on her lap, till Mary stopped shuffling her feet. Lifting her chin, the girl clasped her hands behind her back.

"I'm sorry I was naughty. It was wrong of me to run away and hide from you."

She gulped, then continued in a rush. "Papa says I have to take my punishment from you, since it was you I was bad for."

It was petty of her, Eliza knew, but she wouldn't have been human if she hadn't felt a sneaky satisfaction at seeing the girl who'd upset her so badly shaking in her boots.

Only problem was, she sympathised with Mary. The child rebelled because she missed her mother. Eliza breathed deep, letting go of her anger.

"Goodness, Mary. I've never punished anyone before." Only a beast beat children, Eliza believed, so spanking was out.

"What punishment do you think you deserve?" she asked, turning it back to the child.

Nonplussed, Mary stared at her, mouth agape.

"Something you don't like to do, perhaps," Eliza prompted, when Mary remained lost for words.

"I hate sewing my sampler," she finally blurted out. "Maybe I should have to sew every day when Judy is playing."

A severe punishment indeed, Eliza thought, fighting not to smile. Mary's grubby, untidy sampler was proof of her dislike of it.

"For how long, do you think?"

"Days and days?" Mary sniffed back tears. "I was very naughty."

"You were," Eliza agreed, appearing to think it over.

Wondering if perhaps Mary was in danger of turning the episode into a tale of bravado with herself as heroine, she decided to downplay the punishment, making it thoroughly boring and mundane. An unpleasant chore, hardly worth mentioning.

"However, since you've not been naughty before, let's say half an hour of your very neatest sewing each afternoon for the rest of the week. That's four days, Mary, then on Sunday, you can make your confession to Fr Martinez when we go to church. After that we can put it behind us and say no more about it."

Relieved at being let off more lightly than expected, Mary agreed.

"Now then," Eliza scanned her step-daughter from head to foot. "You've got black from that burnt tree all over you. Off to the bath house with you and we'll get you cleaned up for dinner."

"Why are you being nice to me?" Mary asked a short time later while Eliza combed her freshly washed hair. "Why aren't you mad at me?"

Eliza took her time answering.

"I think it's because I know what it's like to lose someone you love. When my father died, I was so angry with the factory owner for putting profit ahead of safety. Then when my Mama died, I was angry with the doctors for not making her better. And I was angry with my husband, Jason, for doing dangerous work that killed him. I think feeling angry, as you do, is part of grief, Mary. You can't help being angry, so it wouldn't be fair to be mad at you."

Eliza hadn't put her feelings into words before, and was surprised at how right they sounded. Her own heart felt lighter for the insight into her feelings.

"But, you know, dear," she continued thoughtfully. "If you listen to your heart, you'll hear your Mama telling you to look for things that make you happy. She would want you to be happy again, wouldn't she?"

Reaching for a ribbon, Eliza tied off one braid and began plaiting the other.

"Mary, when you put flowers in that pretty cup beside your mother's picture, try to remember happy times with her. And when you say your prayers, tell your Mama the best thing that happens to you each day. She'll be glad to see you trying, and will help you open your heart to being happy again."

And that's good advice for me, too. I need to stop looking back so often, and start looking to the future.

*****

That night when she closed her book and got up to retire to bed, Eliza didn't wait for Sean to come to her. She went up to him and kissed him on the cheek, her face flaming as she did so.

"Goodnight Sean."

He walked her to the door, rewarding her courage with a warm hug, and a barely felt kiss, not on the cheek as usual, but on her lips.

She stepped through the door, then turned back to smile at him.

"You know, Sean? In spite of Mary's escapade today, I'm beginning to feel we are a family. All four of us together."

"As you say, Eliza. Four of us together." He lay a hand lightly on her tummy. "Soon five of us. We are indeed a family."

16

Awakened by the rooster she'd affectionately dubbed Apollo, Eliza felt more energetic and alive than she had for weeks. The morning malaise she'd grown accustomed to was absent, leaving her with an optimistic spring in her step.

"I'm part of a family again", she murmured, heart singing as she recalled the conversation of the night before. "I've found a family, and a home."

She was humming to herself when Sean joined her in the kitchen for breakfast.

"Someone sounds happy." He grinned, wrapping both arms around her and taking his time over his goodmorning kiss. It felt nice to hear a happy woman in his home again. His happy woman.

"Someone is," Eliza leaning back in his arms, placed her hand on his chest where his heart beat strongly against her palm and laughed gaily. "And if someone was to ask me how I feel this morning, I could honestly tell him I feel *well*. Really well."

Although the conversation over breakfast was inconsequential, both were in sunny moods when Sean pushed back his chair and strode out to join Bill and Tommy in the sheep paddock.

"I'll be home for lunch today," he called over his shoulder. "Make a list if you need me to bring anything back from the shop when I go in to collect the mail."

That afternoon Mary's punishment half hour was coming to a close when Eliza heard Sean ride past on his way to stable Prince Valiant.

He's back, she noted, smiling, thinking little of the fact he was later than usual. Mail day was an excuse for Sean to meet up with fellow farmers on a similar mission and exchange news and views. She looked forward to hearing the latest gossip. Sending Mary out to play, Eliza leant against the verandah post to wait for Sean.

One look at his thunderous frown was enough to warn her the cheerful mood of the morning had fled.

"Where are the girls? There's bad news, and I don't want them worried any sooner than need be."

"Playing with their dolls in the summer house."

Eliza gestured towards the rustic shelter Mr Botham, the previous owner of *Wattle Bend*, had built for his wife to sit in on hot days. One glance had been all it took for Mary and Judy to claim it for a playhouse.

"What bad news, Sean?"

Eliza, her heart accelerating its pace, reached blindly for a chair, sitting heavily.

Taking the chair at her side, Sean pulled a letter from his pocket, handing it to her.

"Read this. It's from my lawyer, Henry Wynne."

Without waiting for her to finish the lengthy missive, he exploded, "Bloody Augusta Jackson! She's going ahead with the court case. Henry says she thinks she can smear your reputation and claim you're not a fit mother. She doesn't even know you, Eliza! That damned woman is determined to have her way, regardless of who she tramples on in the process."

Impatiently, he watched Eliza read, sometimes going back to read a passage a second time. The moment she lifted her eyes, he burst into speech.

"There's no dirt she can rake up on you, is there Eliza? She can't make any of those accusations Henry's referring to stick, can she?"

Eliza stared at him, horrified. Had he married her, thinking she might be … No wonder he didn't want her in his bed! Hurt and anger in equal proportions coloured her desperate reply. Sean had to believe her. She couldn't bear to have him think ill of her.

"I'm innocent of all her filthy insinuations, Sean, but how do I go about proving it? I was a respectable wife to Jason, and then a respectable widow, but how do I prove it? I've got no family of my own to vouch for me, and my only friends are those I've made here and on the goldfields." Tears gathered, but she blinked them back. This was not the time for such futile weakness. "Oh, Sean. We married to save your family from being split up. I can't bear the idea I might end up being a dreadful liability instead."

Eliza's impassioned declaration ringing in his ears, Sean shook his head. How stupid of him to think, for even a moment, that Augusta's filth could be true. When everything he'd learned of Eliza's caring nature proclaimed the exact opposite. Of course it wasn't true.

"It shouldn't come to that," he comforted her, "and you're no liability, Eliza. Anything but." Sean took her hand, giving it a reassuring squeeze. "See, there on the last page, Henry's made a list of information to send him, and documents to bring with us to court. There's also a list of suggestions about character references." He read the list, which included the usual birth certificate, marriage and death certificates as well as a list of professional men whose word would be trusted.

"I've got all those certificates," Eliza exclaimed. "I needed to show them to Fr Martinez before we could be married." Thinking more clearly now the initial shock had worn off, she added, "You should speak to Abbot Salvado, Sean. He checked my story with the police when I first arrived in New Norcia. I was worried Tom Griggan might have died, but he didn't. The police can vouch for me too, can't they? As well as the local man here, there's Sergeant Dickson from Southern Cross. I met him when Jason died. He helped me deal with the official investigation into his accident."

"That's right, Lizzie. You see, you're not the unknown nobody you thought you were."

"Your lawyer wants character references." Naturally resilient, Eliza eagerly counted her friends off on her fingers.

"Will people like George Sampson, Sam Jones and the postmaster do? I can write to them and ask them to help."

Then she remembered one whose word would surely carry extra weight.

"There's Reverend Morton, too, Sean. I attended the services he held for the miners, and he conducted Jason's funeral. If he's still there, his word ought to be good."

"Write to them tonight, and I'll get your letters in the post tomorrow."

*****

By the date set for the court hearing, Sean had acquired letters attesting to both his and Eliza's good character from every person of standing for twenty miles around, as well as some from before he and Ann moved north. Abbot Salvado and Fr Martinez had sent letters of their own directly to Mr Henry Wynne. A few days earlier, Eliza had received a letter from George Sampson in which he told her,

" and so, Eliza, after reading your letter, I made a list of my own of people whose word might count for something, including those whom you mentioned, then went to all of them myself, waiting while they wrote what was required. Only then did I take these letters and post them myself, directly to the lawyer, Henry Wynne. Sergeant Dickson insisted on sending his through official channels, but I watched to see him put it in the mailbag.

I hope all goes well with the hearing, Eliza, and that you and your new husband prevail. Let me know how you get on. "

"Oh, Sean. George is so good. I do hope his efforts on our behalf are sufficient."

*****

It was a very nervous little family who entered the court room behind their lawyer. The children, clean and neat in new Sunday-best dresses and the shiny, new, well-fitting shoes Eliza had bought for them, sat demurely between their father and step-mother, on their best behaviour.

Encountering the Jacksons outside, the girls had greeted their grandfather with hugs and kisses, but had cringed away from their grandmother, to her great annoyance. Her nose in the air, Augusta had swept past them, a victorious smirk on her face, considering victory a foregone conclusion. Humphrey, torn between long friendship for Sean and loyalty to his wife, looked miserably uncomfortable.

They all rose while the magistrate entered and took his place.

"The first case on my list is a child custody dispute between Mr and Mrs Humphrey Jackson and Mr and Mrs Sean O'Grady. Mr Curtis, I see your clients are applying for custody of their two granddaughters."

He scanned the seats behind the lawyers' tables, his gaze settling on the O'Grady family. Eliza shivered, feeling his piercing gaze rest on her before passing on to the children.

"Yes, Your Honour."

"Removing children from their parents is a very serious business, Mr Curtis. Upon what grounds do your clients take this action?"

"On the grounds the children's father is an unfit parent, Your Honour." He went on to give details of how Sean had left his children in the care of an Aboriginal woman.

"My clients, the children's grandparents, feel they are better placed to give their granddaughters an appropriate upbringing." He was prepared to go on at greater length on the subject, but the magistrate interrupted.

"Mr Wynne, what say you to these allegations?"

"That was the situation, Your Honour, until recently. Due to the unexpected nature of his wife's accidental death, Mr O'Grady had no option other than calling on the services of his housekeeper, a woman of unquestionable good character despite the colour of her skin, in caring for Mary and Judith while engaged in working his farm. He tried, unsuccessfully, to employ a governess. However, the situation has now been satisfactorily resolved with Mr O'Grady's recent marriage to the widowed Mrs Baker."

"Is there any other reason to consider Mr O'Grady an unfit parent, Mr Curtis?"

At the lawyer's negative reply, the magistrate's next question sounded quite terse.

"That being the case, Mr Curtis, why have your clients persisted with their petition?"

"Because I won't have that goldfield hussy looking after my granddaughters!"

Butting into the legal questions and answers, Augusta Jackson jumped to her feet, gesturing wildly in Eliza's direction.

"Madam! Sit down!" Thundered the magistrate.

Outraged, Augusta protested, but the magistrate was having none of that.

In his courtroom, he ruled supreme.

"Mr Curtis, control your client, or I'll have her removed."

"Yes, Your Honour."

Humphrey pulled Augusta down onto her seat, whispering urgently, with John Curtis reinforcing his exhortations. As soon as order was restored, the proceedings continued.

"Mr Curtis, upon what grounds do your clients claim Mrs Eliza O'Grady an unfit parent?"

"Ah, umm. She is reported to have come from a life on the Southern Cross goldfields. Nothing is known of her antecedents, and my clients fear she may be a woman of ill-repute."

A hiss of protest from Eliza had Mr Wynne turning in his seat to signal her to be quiet. A quick wink and half smile reassured her a little, and she remembered his satisfaction with all the letters her friends had written on her behalf.

"Can you provide proof to substantiate that claim, Mr Curtis?"

"Ah ... No, Your Honour."

"So, let me get this straight, Mr Curtis. With no evidence whatsoever, your clients dare to defame this young woman's character?"

Mr Curtis, aware of the weakness of the Jackson's claim, hung his head, mumbling a reply.

"These are serious allegations, Mr Curtis. Your clients are in danger of laying themselves open to charges of slander if they cannot prove their accusations."

Turning aside from Mr Curtis, the magistrate centred his attention upon Mr Wynne.

"What do you have to say on behalf of your client, Mr Wynne?"

"Quite a lot, Your Honour, and, unlike my colleague here, I come provided with proofs. Far from being unknown, these documents prove Mrs Eliza O'Grady is exactly who she asserts she is."

He passed over the folder of official documents Eliza had given to him earlier.

"Then, Your Honour, I have a goodly number of letters testifying to Mrs O'Grady's good character, and, indeed, Mr O'Grady's as well. For your convenience I have indexed them and appended brief summaries of the author and contents of each."

A substantial sheaf of letters followed the documents.

Placing a pair of *pince-nez* spectacles on his beaky nose, the magistrate took his time perusing the paperwork with which he'd been presented. Finally, he looked up, addressing Eliza directly.

"Mrs O'Grady, step forward, please. All your identification documents are in order, however, in the interests of thoroughness, I have a number of questions which I feel you are better placed to answer than your lawyer, Mr Wynne."

Quaking in her pretty buckled shoes, Eliza approached the desk. Henry Wynne took his place at her side in case she needed advice.

"Keep your answers brief and to the point," he whispered. "Don't get upset or waffle on."

That was all he had time for before the interrogation began.

"It says in this letter from Mrs Worthington, a first-class passenger on the ship in which you sailed to Western Australia last year, and also the one from Captain MacPherson, the ship's Master, that during the voyage you participated in conducting a school for the children on board. How did that come about, Mrs O'Grady?"

Mrs Worthing! And Captain MacPherson! Eliza gaped in amazement. Later Henry Wynne explained to her that he knew Mrs Worthington, and recalling which ship she had travelled home from England on, had approached her.

"She remembered you well, my dear," he explained. "As for the captain, I read in the shipping news that his ship was once again in Freemantle, so paid him a visit."

But that explanation came after they left the court. Now, with the magistrate waiting on an answer, Henry Wynne nudged her to pay attention and answer the question she had been asked.

"Oh! Well, Your Honour, when we were at sea, a number of entertainments and educational pursuits were offered to the passengers. Most people joined in, and I chose to help the Chief Stewardess with her children's activities."

"I see. Reverend Morton writes that while on the goldfields, you taught Sunday School to the children of his congregation. What qualifications do you possess, Mrs O'Grady, that lead you to repeatedly offer your services as a teacher?"

"I've had no proper training, Your Honour, but I was well educated myself, and I enjoy the company of children."

"Mr Samuel Jones writes that you worked as his assistant in his general store on the goldfields. An unusual occupation for a woman in such an unruly place, surely?"

"Not so unusual, Your Honour. I held a similar position in a shop in Manchester before I married my first husband, Mr Jason Baker. Mr Jones had trouble keeping an assistant as the men he employed would run off prospecting. That's why he was happy to employ me, Your Honour."

"Umm. He describes you as capable, good at handling money, and scrupulously honest. Those, and words in similar vein, are also used by a number of other men who've testified to your good character, I see. Sergeant Dickson, Reverend Morton and others all describe you as a virtuous wife to Mr Baker, and a caring friend to your neighbours. Do they speak truthfully, Mrs O'Grady?"

"They do, Your Honour."

"Hmm. I see you became separated from your travelling companions when returning from Southern Cross, becoming lost in the bush for a number of days. Careless of you, Mrs O'Grady." He scented a story behind the official account with which he had been furnished, but when Eliza was not forthcoming, he moved on.

"Shepherds from New Norcia rescued you, Abbot Salvado says."

"They saved my life, Your Honour."

"You appear to have entered into your second marriage rather precipitately, Mrs O'Grady. Your first husband had been dead only a matter of weeks."

"I am carrying my first husband's child, Your Honour. It is difficult for a woman with a baby to find respectable employment. When Fr Martinez suggested I accept Mr O'Grady's offer of marriage, like you, I considered it too soon. However, Mr O'Grady's need of a mother for his children was urgent. Our marriage is a mutually beneficial arrangement."

Since that was as much as she was prepared to say on *that* subject, she gave a soft sigh of relief when there were no further questions.

"Very well. Mrs O'Grady, you may return to your place."

Taking his time about it, the magistrate flicked through a few more of the letters in front of him, then took off his spectacles and addressed the Court.

"It is my finding that this case is a malicious waste of the Court's time."

He held aloft the bundle of letters.

"A great number of people, among them some of very high standing, have gone to the trouble of attesting to the good character of both Mr Sean O'Grady and his second wife, Mrs Eliza O'Grady. I can see with my own eyes that these two little girls in front of me are healthy, clean, well-nourished and well-groomed."

He smiled at the girls, then frowning, resumed his discourse.

"It is my opinion that instead of attempting to traduce these parents and deprive them of their children, Mr and Mrs Jackson, you should be giving thanks your grandchildren are in such fine hands. Case dismissed. Mr Curtis, your clients are liable for all expenses."

"No! No! You can't do that! Those children are mine! I have a right to them. Give them to me!"

Literally kicking and screaming, Augusta Jackson was dragged from the courtroom.

Judith, whom Sean had picked up in his arms, buried her face against his shoulder, sobbing in fear.

Feeling a small hand clasp hers tightly, Eliza looked down to see Mary cringing against her, hiding her face in her skirts. Crouching down to the child's level, she whispered comfortingly to the little girl.

"It's alright, Mary dear. It's all over now, and you're safe. No-one can ever take you away from your Papa now."

Trailing well behind the Jacksons, Henry Wynne escorted his clients from the room.

"As soon as I heard who was on the bench today," he told them, "I knew we had nothing to fear. He's a stickler for the law, and a good judge of character. Besides, John Curtis was out of his depth. He should have known better than to bring such a weak case."

"I'd guess Augusta browbeat him into it," Sean replied.

"The Jacksons are important clients of his firm. Thanks to you, Henry, we were better prepared. I can never thank you enough for saving my girls for us."

*****

Outside the courthouse, Humphrey Jackson came up to Sean.

"Before you go, Sean, I want to apologise. I let Augusta have her way in this, with disastrous consequences. I know forgiveness is too much to ask, but I'm begging you, Sean. When the dust settles, could you see your way to allowing me to see Mary and Judith from time to time?"

"Humphrey, as I've said before, you are their grandfather. I know you love them and would not wish to bar my door to you. However, unless Augusta mends her ways, I don't see how I can allow her near Mary and Judith. You saw how she frightens them."

"Your wife is obviously not a well woman, Mr Jackson. Write to us and we'll let you know how the girls go on. Maybe, in time, you can pay a visit," Eliza offered impulsively. She couldn't help feeling sorry for the poor man.

Glancing guiltily at her husband, she was relieved to see his curt nod of agreement.

"Mrs O'Grady, thank you. That is very generous of you, considering ..."

With tears in his eyes, Humphrey made his farewells, both families then setting out for their homes.

17

After the grief, anxieties and fears of the previous weeks, life at *Wattle Bend* felt wonderfully calm and peaceful.

Which was exactly the way Eliza wanted her life to be right now.

Last Sunday Fr Martinez had led the congregation in giving thanks for the O'Grady family's safe deliverance from the threat Augusta Jackson had posed, and every night Eliza also thanked God in her prayers for guiding her to this haven, and for preserving her new family from being torn apart.

For the first few days after their return home, the girls, even independent little Mary, were clingier than normal. Eliza found herself looking for new ways to bring the sunshine back into their lives, her heart warming when she succeeded. Instead of whining when showers prevented them from picnicking in the paddocks with their father, the pretty story she'd spun about the magical properties of the rainbow they saw glowing across the full width of the dark, louring sky had soon led them to hope the wet weather continued.

The letter she had written to Mrs Willoughby had been promptly answered, and so warmly, Eliza knew she had an unexpected new friend in her old shipboard acquaintance. She had admired the older woman on the ship, but, not being in the same social circles as the Willoughbys, had not thought to keep in contact with her after docking in Freemantle.

Other people who had also supported herself and Sean, people much nearer to home, were becoming firm friends too. Sean had taught her to drive the sulky, giving her the freedom to regularly meet up with the other women of the district.

Mary and Judith benefitted too, as their circle of friends expanded. Mary still had difficult moments, but as time went on, they became less frequent.

"You know, darling," Eliza reminded Mary one afternoon when the child had thrown a tantrum, "your Mama will always have her special place in your heart. Always and forever. I can't take that away from her, even if I wanted to. And I don't."

Seeing the child's mutinous expression lightening a little, she had dared to give her a quick, reassuring hug and continue.

"There is a different place for me, but, Mary, our hearts are amazing things. They have lots of room, for lots of people. Loving someone new actually makes your love for those already in your heart even stronger. There is no limit to the number of people you can love."

"Mama used to say I should love everyone. Even Grandmama," Mary said, a little fearfully.

"But I don't. I hate Grandmama. She shouts and hits and says mean things."

Feeling a challenge in this statement, Eliza thought carefully before she answered.

"We should try to love everyone, just as your Mama said, Mary, but some people are harder to love than others."

And that's particularly true of Augusta Jackson.

"Your Grandmama wasn't always the way she is now, you know. She began to feel unwell in her head. That's what makes her so terribly angry all the time. Her doctor says that when your Mama and Papa bought *Wattle Bend*, she missed your Mama dreadfully. Then, after the accident, wanting your Mama back the way she was when she was a little girl, became an obsession. That means she couldn't stop thinking about it," she explained, seeing the question trembling on Mary's lips.

"Her illness made her think you and Judy would do instead, and she tried to take you for her own little girls. Papa and Mr Wynne stopped her from doing that. Your Grandpapa wrote in his letter that the doctor has given her stronger medicine to help her feel better."

"I still hate her. We're not *her* little girls. We're Papa's little girls." Mary thought for a moment, then added very softly, "I guess we're your little girls, too, Mam."

Tears welled in Eliza's eyes, but she wiped them away, smiling brightly.

"You are, Mary darling, and I love you both."

They sat side by side without speaking for several minutes. Stirring herself finally, Eliza knew she had to give the child a way to lay aside the hatred she felt for her grandmother.

Otherwise it would fester in her heart, making her bitter, as no child should be.

"I've been thinking, darling. If you pray to God to help your Grandmama get better, so she'll be nice again, that would be a special way of loving her. It would make your Mama happy, wouldn't it?"

Mary had run off to play without answering, but at bedtime that night Eliza heard her praying, "   and God, please make Grandmama get better again."

*****

"Oh! Oh my!" Eliza exclaimed.

She had been sitting reading quietly with Sean in the sitting room a few evenings later.

"What? Is something wrong, Eliza?"

Dropping his book, Sean stood, uncertain what had caused Eliza's outburst, but ready to offer assistance should it be needed. She had a peculiar, unreadable expression on her face which aroused all his protective instincts.

"No," Eliza laughed breathlessly. "It's the baby, Sean. I felt it move." She rested a gentle hand on her tummy, hoping to feel that amazing flutter kick again.

"Let me feel, too." Eagerly, Sean dropped to his knees beside her chair, placing one of his large, work-roughened hands next to hers. "That is … " He worried he might have overstepped the mark. "That is, if it's all right?"

"Of course it's all right." Eliza pulled back the hand he lifted away, holding it in place.

"There," she breathed. "He did it again. Did you feel it, Sean? My baby's really there. Really alive. Oh, I feel wonderful. This is so exciting."

Sean laughed indulgently at his wife's excitement, then sobered abruptly. He never failed to be awestruck at the miracle of new life, but at this moment he suddenly missed Ann more than he had for weeks. If he didn't look at her face, he could almost imagine the woman carrying this baby was his beloved Ann, as she had been three times during their marriage. They had been such joyous times, filled with love and plans for the future. Plans which had been dashed when she was taken from him. He couldn't bear the pain.

"Sean ...?" Confused, Eliza stared after him. One moment he'd been as excited as herself over the baby, then he'd rushed from the room as if the hounds of Hell were snapping at his heels.

What had happened?

Eliza waited, desultorily pretending to read, her heart growing heavier by the minute. Sean had promised to love her baby as his own. Had he discovered he couldn't? Was that why he'd left so abruptly? She wrapped her arms around herself, around her baby, protecting it, the both of them, from rejection.

With similar interests, mutual respect and love of Sean's children, she'd thought they were settling into their marriage so well. Eliza even admitted to herself she looked forward to the time it would become a proper marriage. As she'd told Mary, she truly believed one could love again. She wasn't there yet, but could see that time ahead of her.

And she'd believed Sean felt the same.

He'd been growing more affectionate with her lately. More trusting. Confiding in her as he hadn't at first. What would she do if she was wrong? What if Sean felt he'd made a mistake? She didn't think she could bear to leave *Wattle Bend* and the two little girls who had stolen her heart.

She waited a while longer, but when her husband didn't return, she put her book aside. Banking the small fire they'd taken to lighting, now the evenings were turning colder, she fixed the fireguard in place and doused the lamps, securing the house for the night.

Lying in bed, she prayed harder than ever for a happy future. Eliza was drifting into a troubled sleep when she heard a voice in her mind she'd thought never to hear again.

Don't give up, Lizzie.

"I won't," she murmured.

*****

When Apollo woke her the next morning, she rose with renewed determination to make her marriage to Sean O'Grady work. Not only her happiness depended on succeeding; her baby's did too.

"Good morning, Sean." Not a trace of her doubts was allowed to shadow her cheerful greeting. "How are you feeling?"

"Better."

Sean walked up to her, wrapping both arms around her and hugging her close to him.

"I'm sorry for last night, Eliza. It wasn't you. I'm really glad I married you, and I'm looking forward to our little one, here," he patted her tummy.

"It's just … Well. Last night, feeling this baby move under my hand brought back memories."

"I guess that's to be expected, Sean," Eliza murmured, warm and reassured within his arms. "I have my own bad moments too, from time to time. But you know, on the whole I'm very happy with you and the girls. I'm looking forward to after Baby is born."

It was true. She didn't think it was love she felt for Sean, but she liked and respected him. And she did miss the pleasures of the marriage bed. Many women had built good marriages from less.

"Me too, Lizzie. I'm looking forward too, to when you become my wife in truth."

If the lusty response of his body was any indication, Eliza knew as he kissed her, that he also spoke the truth.

18

Winter had segued overnight into early Spring. Raising her face to the afternoon sunshine, so welcome after a week of gusty showers, Eliza inhaled the scent of the wattles the farm was named for. The short, bushy trees had exploded into a sea of golden blooms, their perfume filling the air during recent weeks. She sniffed appreciatively. Their scent was spicier than that of the English flowers she'd grown up with, but Eliza loved it.

Earlier that day, she and the girls, both of whom had now fully accepted her as a member of their family, had taken their sketch books on a walk, making drawings of the beautiful wildflowers which brought the drab, dull greens of the bush to vibrant life.

It wasn't only the amazing floral displays which captured Eliza's heart, however.

Lambs and calves were making their appearances in the stock paddocks, and the bush was also alive with new life. It seemed every other tree boasted a nest full of chicks demanding to be fed.

The kangaroos who shared the paddock beside the creek with a flock of sheep, had new joeys hopping in and out of their pouches, and the possum who came begging for fruit on the back verandah at night, had a wide-eyed baby clinging tightly to her back.

Right then Eliza's baby kicked vigorously, reminding her that soon she, too, would have a new little one of her own.

"Any day now," she whispered, rubbing her hand soothingly over the enormous bulge under her apron.

Smiling dreamily, she picked up her sewing. She needed to keep on if she was to have the embroidered coverlet for the baby's crib finished in time.

A quick glance assured her Mary and Judith were still busy playing some complicated game on the front lawn and didn't need her just yet. Watching fondly, she smiled to see Sean's hard-working dogs, who weren't needed to help mend fences today, chasing a ball for the girls.

The glass enclosed section of the front verandah was a lovely sun-trap during cooler days. *Such a pleasant spot,* Eliza thought, yawning, her sewing falling unnoticed to the floor.

I must have dozed off, she thought, sitting up with a start.

That often happened lately. Had it been the girls shouting which woke her?

Anxiously wondering at the ruckus the dogs were kicking up, she hurriedly looked out the window for the girls. Maybe a snake had come into the garden.

If only it had been a snake!

"Joan!" Eliza screamed, racing down the path to the front gate.

The buckboard she'd caught a glimpse of outside the gate, was still in sight, disappearing quickly down the track, Mary and Judy leaning out the back of it.

"Mam! Mam!"

The girls' voices grew fainter as Eliza stood transfixed, leaning heavily on the gate. What was going on?

Was that a woman driving off with the girls, much faster than was either comfortable or safe on the rutted track? Sean had been talking about mending the potholes left by the winter rains, but had yet to get round to it.

"Missus! What you yelling out for? Is it the baby?"

Joan came panting up to join her looking down the track. "That's our girlies. Who they going off with, then?"

By now Eliza was beginning to get her wits about her.

"Come on Joan," she ordered, taking the housekeeper's hand and dragging her round to the stables at a trot, the fastest she could manage, in spite of the urgency.

"I think it must be Augusta Jackson," she gasped. "She's stolen the girls, Joan. You've got to help me get them back. Polly!" she yelled, seeing the other woman unpegging the clothes they'd washed that morning.

"Joan, you take Blackie and ride like the wind to tell the police. If there's no-one in the office, ask Mrs Fraser to send some men after Mrs Jackson. She mustn't be allowed to get away with our girls."

"No fear, Missus. We'll get them back for you." Without waiting to saddle Blackie, Joan threw herself onto the horse's back and set off, riding cross-country for help.

"Polly, help me saddle Billie, then run as fast as you can to where the men are mending the fences in the ten-acre paddock. Tell the Boss. He took Prince today, so he'll be able to go straight after them. Tell him I'm taking Billie and going over the creek to the shortcut out to the main road. If I can, I'll try to stop her before she gets too far."

"Missus, the baby! You better not ride dat horse or you hurt yourself."

"I've got to, Polly. I'll be careful. Go now. Tell the Boss. Quick as you can."

Leading placid old Billie over to the mounting block, Eliza scrambled into the saddle and set off for the creek and the shortcut. It lopped a good three miles off the distance between the farm and the main south-bound road. Too narrow for vehicles, its use was restricted to riders and pedestrians.

Even though she felt awfully uncomfortable astride Billie, Eliza knew she'd never be able to face Sean if she sat twiddling her thumbs, doing nothing while Augusta Jackson kidnapped his daughters.

Riding the shorter route, while the buckboard had to go round the winding roads, Eliza felt she had a reasonable chance of intercepting Augusta. She would have sent either Joan or Polly, except she was certain Augusta would take no notice of them at all. She wasn't sure Augusta would stop for her either, but she could at least point the men who would soon be following her in the right direction.

Refusing steadfastly to think what would happen if she failed, she kicked slow old Billie into a faster gait.

Emerging from the trees near the crossroads, Eliza stared up and down the road. Nothing was in sight. Did that mean she was too late? Almost crying with frustration, Eliza wished she had taken Blackie, only Blackie was a young horse and she'd doubted her ability to control him.

She was still wondering which way to go now, when the distant rumble of wheels from the right direction reached her ears.

Was it them?

Edging Billie forward, she stood in the stirrups trying to see round the corner.

"It is them," she exclaimed as Augusta's buckboard bowled into view, the single horse pulling it already lathered and straining to keep up the rattling pace demanded of it.

Augusta saw her, sitting astride Billie in the middle of the road, at almost the same moment.

Instead of stopping, as Eliza had hoped she would, Augusta whipped her horse up. Afraid of being run down, Eliza moved aside at the last minute, helpless to stop her.

"Mam! Help us Mam!"

It near broke Eliza's heart to hear Mary and Judith crying out to her and be helpless to come to their aid. They'd been clinging for dear life to the wildly rocking vehicle bounding past her in a cloud of dust on the rough road.

Wheeling Billie round, she set off in pursuit.

She didn't have far to follow. In her ill-considered haste, Augusta had caught a wheel in a pothole on the road. The buckboard had tipped, then teetered back onto its wheels, but the horse, rearing in fright, had got a leg over the traces bringing the wagon to an abrupt halt.

Reigning Billie in, Eliza kicked her feet free of the stirrups and slid to the ground.

Mary, quick to see her chance, scrambled down and was already helping her sister to follow her.

"Get back here!" Augusta screamed, abandoning her struggles with the horse. "You girls get back here!"

"Quickly girls. Run and hide," Eliza called, watching fearfully as Augusta jumped to the ground and rushed towards her. Putting herself between the children and their maddened grandmother, she was horrified to see a gun in Augusta's hand.

"Get out of my way, you stupid woman," Augusta yelled waving the deadly weapon about.

"Girls! Come back here! You're mine now, and you shan't escape me."

Raising the pistol, one of Samuel Colt's famed six-shooters, she pointed it at the fleeing children. Desperate, Eliza ran forward, grappling with her for possession of the gun.

Augusta appeared at first oblivious to the thunder of hoofbeats approaching at speed, but not so Eliza. Turning to look, she unconsciously loosened her grip on Augusta's arm. Manically, Augusta turned to face the newcomers, firing wildly just as a party of men led by the police constable from New Norcia arrived on the scene.

"Aargh!" Eliza screamed, falling to the ground, clutching at her arm. "Constable. Be careful."

"Madam! Drop your weapon!" commanded the constable, only to be ignored as Augusta, incensed, turned to confront yet another arrival.

"Eliza! Where are you hurt?" Sean didn't wait for Prince Valiant to come to a standstill. He flung himself down at Eliza's side, cradling her in his arms.

"Keep away from me, or I'll shoot." Augusta held the posse at bay, waving the gun back and forth in front of her.

"You madwoman! You've shot Eliza! You'll swing for this!" Sean bellowed.

"You!" Augusta swung back around, her voice expressing her hatred. Attention now centred fully on her son-in-law, she spewed out her loathing for him.

"You, Sean O'Grady! It's all your fault. If that lily-livered excuse for a man I married had listened to me you'd never have been allowed to marry my daughter. You deserve to die."

She raised the pistol, sighting carefully, determined to take her revenge.

"Sean!"

"Stay still, Eliza."

"No!"

The second shot rang out, reverberating off the hills surrounding them. Eliza's heart stopped, picking up its frantic rhythm again a moment later.

"Sean! Oh, God, Sean," she sobbed.

"Hush, Eliza. I'm alright. She missed me."

Eliza clung to him, fearfully turning to see what was happening.

Obsessed with avenging herself on Sean, Augusta had been oblivious to the constable creeping up behind her. He'd grabbed at her arm, causing her shot to go wide, thus saving Sean's life, and now stood, arms spread wide, held at bay by the gun Augusta waved madly from one to the other of the men confronting her.

"Madam! You're under arrest for attempted murder! Put down that gun before you make it worse for yourself!"

Augusta, wild-eyed, stared around her from one man to another, knowing herself hopelessly outnumbered.

"Worse for myself?" she appeared to suddenly realise her situation.

By now several guns were steadily trained on Augusta, protecting Sean and Eliza from her madness.

Before anyone could move, Augusta screamed wildly. And turned her gun on herself.

This time no-one was close enough to stop her.

This time her aim was true.

19

"Eliza. Oh, Eliza. Thank the Good Lord you're safe." Sean knelt in the dust, cradling his wife tenderly in his arms. He pressed a heartfelt kiss to her forehead.

"Mrs O'Grady," the constable interrupted them. "Were you injured? You cried out."

Looking down, Eliza's vision blurred at the sight of her own blood soaking into her dress. Without Sean's support, she feared she may have fainted.

"My ... My arm. Oh, Sean, it hurts."

In the heat of the moment she'd felt nothing but a sharp stinging sensation. Now the emergency was over, her arm throbbed, the pain nauseating.

Sean grasped her sleeve, ripping the fabric to expose her wound.

"Only a flesh wound, thank God. Leave my wife to me, Constable. I'll take care of her. You take care of Augusta Jackson."

In moments he'd fashioned a pad from the clean handkerchief in his pocket. "Hold that in place, Eliza, while I tear your apron up to make a bandage."

"Sean," Eliza clutched at his arm. "The girls. Where are they? Oh, don't let them see what happened to their grandmother."

She pushed herself up, looking wildly all around.

"Did you see where they went?"

Now Sean was on his feet, poised to rush off in search of his missing children. In all the excitement no-one had remembered why they were chasing Augusta in the first place. Now, those men not occupied in wrapping Augusta's body in a blanket taken from the back of the buckboard, gathered around Eliza and Sean.

"Mary! Judith! It's safe to come back," Eliza called, her own hurts forgotten.

"Girls! Papa's here. Come to me!" Sean echoed her calls.

"Papa?"

All eyes turned to the frightened little face peering from behind a dense bush growing on the roadside.

"Papa, is it really safe? Grandmama was pointing her gun at us. Then we heard shooting."

"It's all over now. Your Mam saved you. You're safe now."

"Judy, Papa's here. We can come out now." Mary called over her shoulder to her sister, and crawled out from under the bush and ran to her throw herself into her father's arms, closely followed by Judith.

"I took good care of Judy, Papa," Mary told him, burrowing her face into his shoulder.

"When Grandmama grabbed us and put us in her wagon, I made Judy hold on tight so we didn't fall out when we hit the bumps."

Now she knew herself to be safe, Mary was quickly recovering her usual ebullience.

"Mam!"

Judith, tears running down her pale cheeks, flung herself into Eliza's arms, eliciting a squeak of pain.

"Mam, you're bleeding." She reached out tentative fingers to the blood covering the front of Eliza's dress.

"Did Grandmama shoot you with her gun?"

"Yes, she did."

Sean, his daughter's question reminding him his wife still awaited his attention, hugged Judith, gently moving her aside. "I need to finish bandaging your Mam's arm, then I'll see about getting all my precious girls home."

The warmth in his eyes as he gazed at Eliza left her in no doubt, she counted as one of his 'precious girls'. Dropping her eyes, she felt warmth spread throughout her being.

"Is the babe alright, Lass?"

Mr Fraser, shielding the girls from the sad work being carried out behind him, ran an assessing gaze over the young woman in whom he took a proprietary interest, his having been the home which had sheltered her on her arrival in New Norcia.

Right on cue, the baby kicked a tattoo, signalling to Eliza that all was well.

In the end, it was decided Sean should take his family home in Augusta's buckboard while Billie was borrowed to carry Augusta's shrouded body back to the police station. The men were swinging into their saddles when one last player appeared on the scene.

Recognising Sean, Humphrey rode straight up to him.

"Sean, have you seen Augusta? She escaped from Mrs Brearley's care, and I've tracked her heading in this direction."

Heart groaning at the onerous task fate had laid upon him, Sean climbed back down. Taking Humphrey aside, he explained the events of the afternoon. Taking the now weeping man in his arms, Sean patted his back.

"Now, man. Don't be taking on so," he murmured. "It's none of it your fault, and nothing to be done about any of it now."

"Of course. Of course, you're right, my boy. I should have been more vigilant, but she'd been as good as gold. I thought it safe to make a trip down to Perth. Never in my worst imaginings would I have believed her capable of this."

"Am I right in thinking you're this unfortunate woman's husband?"

The constable had dismounted and come to stand at Sean's elbow.

"Yes. Yes, Constable. You'll need me to sort things out, I expect. I'll come with you immediately. Oh, dear," he mopped at his eyes.

"My poor Augusta. She was such a bonny girl."

"Mr Jackson?" At Eliza's call, the men turned as one to look at her. "Mr Jackson, when you've finished in town, you're to come to us. That's right, isn't it, Sean?" she added belatedly.

"Yes, of course, my dear," he agreed. "We'll be expecting you for dinner, Humphrey."

"Thank you, my dear Mrs O'Grady. That's very generous of you, considering …"

"You're family, Mr Jackson."

And, in Eliza's opinion, it was time to begin mending fences. For the sake of the girls.

As Augusta's escort walked their horses sedately down the road, Sean ran after Mr Fraser, the last in line.

"Angus," he called, "Would you go to Mrs turner, the midwife, you know, and ask her to pay Eliza a visit. For my peace of mind. She's very near her time, and after today, … Well. I'd just feel better about her."

"Certainly, Sean. It'll give me an excuse to escape this miserable cortege. It's been a bad business. A bad business."

*****

The ecstatic welcome from not only Joan and Polly, but the whole Smith family, had finally subsided. Some time had elapsed since Sean had delivered Eliza, Mary and Judith home, and still neither Humphrey nor Mrs Turner had yet arrived. Deciding to wait their own meal on the arrival of their guests, Eliza had given the children theirs, and was now tucking them up in their beds.

"Goodnight Mama," Judith murmured sleepily, returning Eliza's kiss.

Dreading the outcry she expected from Mary at her sister's slip-up, Eliza held her breath. So weary she wasn't sure she could cope with a scene right now, she allowed a tiny moan of protest to escape her lips. Her back ached so dreadfully she was afraid she'd harmed herself riding after Augusta. Resignation dragging at her heart, she turned to Mary, but the child surprised her.

"You came after us today," the girl said in a tiny voice. "You stopped Grandmama from shooting at us when we ran away from her, and then she shot you instead. You were just like a real mother."

"Yes, well," Eliza sank down onto Mary's bed, reaching out to clasp the girl's hand in her own. "Maybe that's because I am a real mother, and you and Judy are my little girls just as much as the baby I'll be having soon."

"How can we be your little girls? We weren't your babies."

"No, but I love you with all my heart, and I always will. We don't have to be the same blood for me to love you."

Mary thought over her answer carefully.

"I … I love you, too," she whispered. "I'd like you to be my mother, just like my real Mama. Can I call you Mama instead of Mam?"

"Oh, darling. That would make me so happy. If it's what you really want, Mary, dear." Eliza's eyes filled as she hugged her daughter.

"I do want it. Goodnight Mama."

Mary's arms returning Eliza's hug were so tight she felt painfully uncomfortable, but with her heart overflowing with love, Eliza didn't mind in the slightest.

"Goodnight, Mary darling."

*****

"Hello!"

Humphrey's call, and the sound of horses and sulky wheels outside sent Eliza hurrying from the girl's bedroom to stand with Sean on the verandah to welcome their guests.

"I met Mrs Turner, here, just down the track a-ways," Humphrey explained, handing the woman down from her sulky. "You go on in, Mrs Turner. I'll see to your horse."

"I'll give you a hand, Humphrey." Sean picked up the reins and led the equipage round the side of the yard to the stables, Humphrey following with his horse, and old Billie whom he'd been leading, his services no longer needed.

"Dinner will be ready just as soon as you've refreshed yourselves," Eliza said, leading Betty Turner inside.

"Before we eat, Eliza dear, I'll just check you over after your ordeal. It's why I'm here, after all. How are you feeling?"

"I hope I took no serious hurt from my ride today. I was very mindful of the baby, but oh, Betty, I'm so tired and I ache all over. Especially my back."

The midwife pursed her lips, eyeing her hostess thoughtfully.

In Eliza's bedroom, Betty Turner examined her patient carefully.

"Everything seems in order, Eliza. Your adventures don't appear to have done any harm. You are quite fit, and your baby's heart is beating very strongly. However, unless I'm mistaken, you've begun labour," she said, smiling at Eliza's gasp, "and after all the babies I've delivered, I think I can be relied on to know what's what. Good thing Sean sent for me early."

"But … But I haven't had any contractions, or anything!"

"It's very early stages yet, but my guess is, you'll have that babe at your breast by breakfast."

*****

Betty was not mistaken. Neither in her diagnosis, nor the timing, and, as the kookaburras down by the creek laughed loud and long, welcoming the new day, Eliza heard her daughter's cry for the first time.

Betty prepared mother and child for visitors, then Joan, who had ably assisted her throughout the night, stuck her head round the door, grinning triumphantly at Sean and Humphrey.

On hearing the unmistakeable wail of a newborn, they had abandoned their pacing in the sitting room to wait impatiently in the hall outside Eliza's bedroom.

"Hey, Boss. You got another little girly. A right pretty one, with hair the colour of wattle."

"Eliza …?"

"The Missus good, Boss. Both good."

"Come in, Sean," Betty called. "Come and meet your daughter."

But Sean went to his wife first, leaving Humphrey to peer over Betty's shoulder for a glimpse of the baby.

"Are you really all right, Lizzie?"

"Yes. Yes, I am, Sean," Eliza yawned. "Tired, but very much all right. Come and say hello to Danielle."

"Danielle?"

"Umm." Eliza kissed the tuft of blonde hair on top of the baby's head, then held her out to Sean.

"Isn't she beautiful, Sean?"

Her husband nodded, emotion robbing him of his breath.

"I hope you don't mind my naming her myself, Sean," Eliza said, nervously pleating the edge of the sheet.

"I decided to name her after three of the best men I know. She's O'Grady for you, of course, and Jason's middle name was Daniel, hence Danielle. I'm adding Georgia in the middle for our good friend George Sampson."

"Danielle Georgia O'Grady. Sounds about perfect to me, Lizzie."

Eliza's tired smile was brighter than the ray of morning sunshine peaking between her curtains.

20

"You know who your Mama is, don't you darling girl?" Eliza murmured, dropping a kiss on Dani's head as she lifted the baby to her shoulder.

It wasn't often she got to enjoy time alone with her baby. Dani - the shortened name first used by the children and now adopted by the entire household – was everybody's darling. She had only to raise her voice to announce she was awake to have either her sisters, Joan or Polly hurrying into her nursery. Eliza had had to be very firm with Mary and Judy about not picking her up, but they were always begging to be allowed to sit and cuddle her, or push the pram around the garden. Even Peter and Paul often shyly lined up for a turn at pushing the pram.

It was certainly better by far than her step-sisters being jealous of the new arrival, but Eliza did like to steal a moment purely for herself from time to time. Her tummy full, Dani was ready for her bath. Polly would be along in a minute with the pail of warm water, and then Mary and Judy would sidle through the nursery door as if drawn by a magnet.

Bathtime was fun for all of them, especially Dani who kicked and splashed with obvious enjoyment.

The barking out by the front gate was the first indication of visitors, then the rattling of wheels and clop of hooves sent Eliza to the window to see who it was. She was expecting Betty Turner to drop by when she had time. Eliza and Dani were both due for a final check over from the midwife to see neither had suffered any unpleasant after-effects from the birth several weeks earlier.

Eliza's cheeks grew hot and there was a fluttering of nerves in her stomach.

If Betty pronounced her fit, which she fully expected her to do, then there would be no reason she and Sean need wait any longer to make their marriage real in every respect.

Eliza didn't know if she was ready, but this was the time they had agreed on, months earlier. She did so much want to build a successful marriage with Sean. She had grown to like and respect him. More than like him, she thought, her cheeks flaming hotly.

And, also, she trusted Sean implicitly. He'd kept every one of the promises he'd made her, even though she was aware some of them, this prolonged period of getting to know each other in particular, were not easy for him. She'd been married long enough the first time round to understand the meaning of his body's reactions when her held her close.

She would never have refused him if he'd insisted, but he'd only allowed their intimacies to go so far. These last weeks - the butterflies in her stomach fluttered their wings again – she had noticed an extra warmth in his embraces.

He also had an eager gleam in his eyes when they rested on her once again slender body.

Sometimes when Sean held her in his strong arms and kissed her, she didn't want to wait a single moment longer. At others, her courage ebbed, and she was glad he was not yet sharing her bed.

Jason, whose image was no longer sharp and fresh in her memory, was the only man she had ever lain with.

What if she couldn't give herself as freely to Sean?

What if she froze up in his arms?

What if he compared her to his Ann, and found her wanting?

She rested a hand on her belly, as if to quell the slight queasiness her nerves engendered.

But there was no need to get herself all worked up just yet.

Betty Turner's dusty, hard-worked sulky was a far cry from the brand spanking new equipage turning in through the gate young Pete Smith held open today.

Eliza leaned forward, trying to catch a glimpse of the driver's face. Shaded by a wide-brimmed hat, his bearded face was too shadowed to recognise, but Eliza got a clear sighting of the woman perched up beside him.

At first glance, Eliza thought her a stranger, then suddenly she gasped. It couldn't be …

Not dressed so finely, as if she had just stepped out of the finest emporium catering to ladies of fashion!

Popping Dani back into her cradle with the merest of apologetic kisses, Eliza rushed outside, running up to the side of the carriage.

"Maisie! Maisie Baddams! Is that really you? I barely recognised you, dressed so fine. Come down so I can give you a hug. Oh, Maisie, I'm that glad to see you, but whatever are you doing here?"

This fashionably attired lady, her grey hair tucked up under a hat that seemed to bear a whole garden of impossibly hued roses, looked vastly different to Eliza's friend from the diggings.

Last time Eliza had seen Maisie Baddams she'd been dressed in a rough but serviceable black skirt, scuffed boots and man's blue work shirt, serving plates of stew to hungry miners in her canvas and tin cookhouse.

Lace-trimmed petticoats notwithstanding, Maisie scrambled down, not waiting for a helping hand, to clasp Eliza to her ample bosom.

"I'm that glad to see you, too, Eliza."

"Have you got a hug for me, too, Lizzie girl?"

Laughter lurked in the soft masculine tones.

Eliza looked over her friend's plump shoulder, her mouth opening wide in her amazement.

"George!" she squealed, wriggling free to fall into George Sampson's arms. But this finely-dressed toff wasn't George Sampson as she knew him!

"George? You and Maisie ...?"

"That's right, Lizzie girl. Me and Maisie have tied the knot. We're on our honeymoon and thought to come and see how you're going on."

"Married!" Eliza squealed again, and another round of hugs and kisses ensued.

George, self-consciously straightening the cravat he had yet to grow accustomed to, looked curiously about him, smiling broadly at the melee of children and dogs encircling them.

"Looks like you've got yourself quite a family here."

"A wonderful family, George." Eliza laughed, and began introducing them

"These are my very good friends, Mr and Mrs Sampson. George, Maisie, these two girls are my daughters, Mary and Judith. Judy. Their friends," she pointed to the dark-skinned boys shuffling their bare feet in the dust, "are Peter and Paul Smith."

By this time Joan and Polly, emerging from the kitchen, had sidled closer, agog at all the excitement.

"Here are their mother and aunt, my good friends Joan and Polly Smith who help me in the house."

The two women bobbed their heads, hands hidden beneath their aprons.

"Oh," Eliza concluded. "And the dogs, of course. Snapper and Jump. The men are all out in the paddocks."

"Hey, Mister," Pete tugged on George's coat. "Kin I take care of your horse?"

"Well, as to that, I'm not exactly sure …"

"Don't be silly, George. You're staying, and that's that. You didn't come all this way to turn around and leave as soon as you arrived. Hand down those bags, then the boys can take your horse and carriage round to the stables."

"Lizzie?" Maisie slipped her arm through Eliza's, accompanying her up the path. "Forgotten someone in all the excitement, haven't you? You wrote about a new baby?"

"Dani. She'll be wondering where I've got to."

Eliza hurried through the door. Sure enough, Danielle was protesting loudly at being left out.

"Come and meet her, Maisie. She's such a little sweetheart."

It wasn't until much later, after Maisie and George had had their fill of cuddles and little Dani, yawning tiredly, had closed her eyes, that Eliza was able to put the baby down for her afternoon sleep and finally be a good hostess, plying her guests with tea and scones spread with the strawberry jam she'd made herself.

"You can't imagine how very happy I am to see you both," she began, to be interrupted by George, chuckling self-consciously.

" but you want to know what we're doing here all dressed up to the nines like a pair of toffs."

"Well … Since you mention it …?"

"I did it, Lizzie. What me and your Jason were aiming for. I hit the jackpot."

"George! You never!"

"I sure enough did, Lizzie. Enough gold to set myself up for life, and this time I won't be frittering it away. Maisie here will see to that."

"Ooh, George. That's so exciting." Smiling widely, Eliza clapped her hands together.

"Yes." His face clouded. Casting his eyes down, he mumbled, "Pity it didn't come sooner. Soon enough to have saved Jason."

"Don't blame yourself, George." Eliza reached over, clasping his hands warmly.

"You mustn't ever do that. Jason made his own decision to be a miner, and I was right there supporting him. What happened was an accident. No-one's fault."

Silence reigned for a moment, all three of them thinking of the man they'd lost.

"So," Eliza asked, determined to restore the happier mood, "tell me how you and Masie come to be together, George. I always thought you were a confirmed bachelor."

She winked at Maisie, to be answered by a self-conscious smirk.

"I'd had my eye on Maisie here for quite a while, Lizzie, only she vowed she'd never get involved with a good-for-nothing miner. Reckoned none of us had the sense to hang onto what we found and build something for the future."

"Mob of bloomin' wastrels, most of them," Maisie corroborated.

"People like me and Sam Jones and his boys, we had the right idea. There's more money to be made supplyin' the miners with what they need than there is grubbin' in the dirt."

"I agree," Eliza smiled. "So what happened to change your mind about George?"

"I had the sense to take my good fortune and pledge myself to following Maisie's lead," George answered, speaking for himself.

"We're going to buy a pub down in Perth. I'll look after the bar, and Maisie will run the dining room. We'll provide good, clean rooms for farming folks like yourself and your new husband when they come to town. With Maisie's business sense, I reckon we can't go wrong."

"It sounds as if you've thought it all out. And, George, Perth isn't far away. We'll be able to visit each other every now and then. Oh, I'm so happy for you both."

*****

Later, while Maisie had a little lie down to recover from the journey, Eliza and George strolled arm-in-arm in the garden.

"I can see you're happy for me and Maisie, young Lizzie, but what I didn't like to ask in front of Maisie and those servants of yours is, are you happy for yourself? 'Cause if you're not, you can pack your bags and come along back to Perth with us. You and little Dani."

"I am happy, George," Eliza assured him, squeezing his arm affectionately. "Sean is a good man. You'll see that for yourself when you meet him. I've settled in here at *Wattle Bend*, you know. It's home, now."

Eliza gazed happily about her, admiring her home.

"Mary and Judy are my daughters," she continued, "and I love them. And Sean," she faltered, a blush staining her cheeks. "Sean is my husband, George, and I love him, too."

She felt uncomfortable saying this to George when she had not yet said it to Sean. Then she wondered if George might think her disloyal to his friend, and hastened to add, "It's different to the way I loved Jason, but it's just as real. I think our marriage is going to be strong. True."

If I have anything to do with it, it will be, she vowed silently, and she would tell Sean how she felt. Just as soon as an opportunity offered itself.

They walked on towards the rose garden planted by Mrs Botham before she sold *Wattle Bend* to Sean. George snapped a pink bud from the bush, handing it to Eliza.

"You and Jason were special to me," he said, "and I feel sought of responsible for you and his baby, Eliza. There's plenty of money to take care of you both. If things don't work out the way you hope, and you ever need a refuge, promise you'll come to me. I just wish I could have made this offer back then, when you did need help."

"I found help, George. I'm happy. Please don't go feeling guilty. And remember, when I did ask you for help with those letters, you came through splendidly. Our lawyer said they really helped the judge make up his mind in our favour. Sean and I were ever so grateful for your help then."

21

Late that same evening Eliza burped Dani after her last feed of the day and lay her gently in her cradle. Straightening, she heard a rustle behind her. Turning, she saw Sean hovering in the doorway, and smiled at him, lifting a finger to her lips. She turned the nightlight down low and followed her husband from the nursery.

"Eliza ... " He hesitated, as if unsure of himself, something Eliza wasn't used to seeing in this man she'd married. "Eliza," he began again, "I need to talk to you." He glanced down the hall to the closed door of the best guestroom. "Will you come out onto the verandah for a few minutes?"

"Of course." Assailed by doubt, Eliza led the way, Sean following closely on her heels. Was something wrong? He'd sounded as if something was wrong, but she couldn't imagine what. Had he objected to her friends arriving so unexpectedly? Surely not.

By the time she turned to face him on the moonlit verandah, a frown pleated a deep crease down her forehead.

"Sean … "

"Give me a minute Eliza. Let me have my say, then I'll listen to what you have to say."

Sick with dread, Eliza nodded, and moved a step away from him.

"Tonight, while you and Maisie were reading to the girls, George and I took our cigars and port outside. You were right about George Sampson being a good friend to you and Jason, Eliza. He is."

So why do I feel as if something dreadful is about to happen?

Eliza wrung her hands.

"George told me about his good fortune, Eliza. He said he wished he could have supported you and Dani after Jason died. He didn't have the means then, but he has now. He told me, that if we were not happy with our arranged marriage, you have a home to go to with him and Maisie."

Avoiding Eliza's agonised gaze, Sean leaned on the verandah railing, breathing heavily. Finally, when his wife said not a word, he turned to look at her.

"You needed a home. That's what you married me for, but now you have another option. Do you want to go with them when they leave, Eliza? I won't stand in your way if you do?"

In a voice so low Eliza wasn't sure she heard him correctly, he added, "A good thing we waited to consummate the marriage. Make it easier to have it annulled."

Annulled? Annulled!

Eliza fell into the nearest chair in an undignified heap. Sean wanted to annul their marriage? She shivered, an icy chill sweeping through her. Frozen, she couldn't have moved if her life depended on it.

"D…d…do you want that, Sean? D…do you want me to leave? D … do you want to annul our marriage?"

"No, damn it, Eliza. I don't want you to go! Or annul our marriage!"

The heated words burst from him. Words which, even fraught with fear as she was, Eliza was certain came from his heart. Words which released her to fight for what *she* wanted. But he hadn't finished.

"This isn't about what *I* want, Eliza. This is about doing what's right for *you*! I took advantage of your vulnerable situation for my own selfish reasons. Now I have to set you free to choose for yourself."

"All right." Eliza spoke slowly, picking her words with care.

Damn George for his interference.

"If I'd had this option back in March, I might not have agreed to marry you, but I didn't have it," Eliza said, choosing to be scrupulously honest.

"We did marry, Sean. I've been your wife for almost six months. In that time, I've learned to love your daughters like my own. They *are* my daughters, too, Sean. *Wattle Bend* is my home, and I love it. And in that time I've come to know you, too, Sean. I respect you for the good man you are; as this conversation proves you to be. I like you." She took a steadying breath, recalling the vow she had made just that afternoon.

"I love you, Sean O'Grady."

She stared him in the eye, heartened by the hope she saw spring to life in his depths of his eyes.

"Be very sure of what you're sayin', Eliza," he warned, reaching for her hands to draw her up to stand chest-to-chest with him. "Be very sure, because I'll only offer you your freedom this once."

"I love you, Sean," she repeated again, more positively than before. "Being your wife, the mother of your children, is all the freedom I want. Now I'm asking you, Sean O'Grady, Do you want me to go? Or stay?"

"Oh, Lizzie," Sean crushed her to him, her breasts aching from being squashed so tightly.

"Stay with me, Lizzie darlin'. Stay with me forever."

He moved her away from him the tiniest fraction, so his lips could claim hers in a searing kiss. Rising onto her toes, Eliza plastered herself against Sean's chest, claiming him as thoroughly as he claimed her. Reaching up to take his hair in two firm hands, she held him to the kiss when he would have pulled away.

"Eliza. Eliza, my darling," he murmured when they finally came up for air. "I love you too, my brave girl."

"Not so much brave as desperate," she murmured back, chuckling softly. "You were all set to do what you saw as the right thing, and send me away, weren't you?"

Keeping her close, Sean nodded. "I did believe giving you your freedom was right. Honourable. Still do."

Men! Eliza huffed. *Men and their stupid, noble honour they let come between them and their happiness.*

"Which is why I had to make you understand *Wattle Bend* and this family are *my* home. *My* family. That's all I've ever asked for, Sean. A home and family to call my own. And I've found both here. With you."

"They're yours, Lizzie darling. For as long as we live."

It was some time later when Sean once again lifted his lips from Eliza's.

"I'd better let you go," he whispered, reluctance in every syllable, "or Dani will be awake, demanding her Mama and you'll not have had any sleep."

"Then come with me, my love," Eliza whispered back.

"Are you sure?"

"Very sure. I'm completely healed. Completely ready to show my husband how welcome he is in my bed. Come."

And Sean went with her, completing her happiness.

THE END

I hope you enjoyed reading *Home is the Heart*.

If you have enjoyed reading Home is the Heart, perhaps you'd like to leave a review on Amazon, Goodreads or whichever site you prefer, to help other readers find my books.

Reviews are also a really great way for readers to connect with authors.

To get Lena's new books as soon as they're released – go to

www.lenawestauthor.com

and make sure that you are signed up for news and release notices!

About the Author

Born in tropical North Queensland, Lena loves living close to the sea, although she moved frequently during her early years, living everywhere from large cities to isolated farms. Her most recent home has a deck overlooking the water, which is her favourite room in the house.

After working as a teacher, she took early retirement to travel Australia in a motorhome. This idyllic lifestyle lasted several years, during which time she indulged in the creation of story plots and their settings, culminating with the fulfillment of her lifelong ambition to write.

Storytelling came naturally - she had been making up stories for her own entertainment all her life, but it wasn't until she began traveling that she made time to write down some of her favourites. *Marrying Alan Morgan*, is the first in a series of rural romances set in the fictional town of Oxley Crossing. She also writes standalone Australian contemporary and historical romances.

With an addiction to happily-ever-afters, in both her reading and writing, the romance genre was a natural fit, and the variety of places she has lived have all added to the settings in which she brings love to life.

You can find Lena on Facebook at:

https://www.facebook.com/LenaWestAuthor/

or sign up for her newsletter at:

www.lenawestauthor.com

Other Books by
Lena West

Historical Romances

 **Unto Death**

In Colonial society of the 1860s marriage is a contract unto death; and scandal is death of another kind.

https://www.amazon.com/dp/B07D3MZ1L4

 **Emily's baby**

In the 1950s an unwed mother needed help if she was to keep her child. Emily had no family, and no money, but she would do whatever it took to keep her precious baby.

https://www.amazon.com/dp/B07TPDN13W

Contemporary Romances

 **Loving Fenella**

When artist and teacher, Fenella Wilkins, is inspired to paint Greg Kendall, she falls in love with both him and his daughter, Aimee. But he is engaged to the beautiful model, Linda Beck. It is against Fen's principles to poach another woman's man, even when self-centred Linda is the other woman.

https://www.amazon.com/dp/B07B3RLS98/

 **Forgotten**

When a soldier returns from the front minus his memory, is he the same man he was when he left? How can Krista be sure which man she really loves?

https://www.amazon.com/dp/B083Y2ZR28

Contemporary Series

Love in Oxley Crossing Series

In the rural town of Oxley Crossing, love is in the air, and romance triumphs, no matter the challenges.

 **Marrying Alan Morgan**

Sparks fly when a feisty red-haired city girl with a past that makes it hard to trust, meets a bitter, disillusioned farmer who's sure love isn't worth the effort. But sometimes, the heart knows better than the mind.

https://www.amazon.com/dp/B0774V1L25/

 **Saving Jonathon Armitage**

A woman come home for family, a man sworn to moving on, jealousy, distrust and misdirection, a life transformed by love.

https://www.amazon.com/dp/B0788GCQJQ

 **Finding Mr Wright**

Escaping her violent ex-husband by claiming sanctuary in Oxley Crossing is the best decision Geni Sullivan has ever made – for herself and her son, nine-year-old Jamie.

https://www.amazon.com/dp/B07C98B7PJ

 **Electing Robert Whitman**

At the second wedding in a matter of months, Sophie James is seated next to the man she had a teenage crush on. A single, unattached man to whom she is still very attracted. When she returns to The Crossing to help her mother, she decides to take a chance on him.

https://www.amazon.com/dp/B07KWKLJG6

 **Redeeming Josh Marten**

Opposites attract when vibrant, outgoing Thea Benson meets withdrawn, curmudgeonly sculptor, Josh Marten, but behind her bubbly image, Thea is not who she appears to be.

https://www.amazon.com/dp/B07RNHBYG7

 **The Making of Joey Lambert**

It is said strong women are not simply born; they are made that way by the storms they walk through. Sienna Smith has survived a category five personal cyclone, but at tremendous cost. One step at a time she's clawed her way back, however, she believes that last difficult step, the one back to 'normal', is beyond her. Not even love for kind, gentle Joey Lambert can carry her that far.

https://www.amazon.com/dp/B088D6RHKD

Connect with Lena!

Be the first to know about it when Lena's next book is released!

Sign up to Lena's newsletter at

www.lenawestauthor.com